I0736813

VOLCHIN & OTHER STORIES

Graduating from Keele University with a PhD in Pure Maths and a pocketful of prizes and commendations for short stories of an unsettling nature, Clark Nida's career went on to be nothing if not diverse.

He has acted in pantomimes, engineered software, sold encyclopaedias, been a mental health nurse, a police scientist and a senior academic. He has lived, worked and travelled widely overseas in Europe, Scandinavia, and the USA (which, as a resident alien living in five-star hotels, run-down motels and way-out alternative communities, he has seen more of than most Americans ever do).

He now lives in Whitby, on the brow of Yorkshire's Jurassic Coast, with a virtual cat, a pet geode and a 350-year-old ghost of himself.

by the same author

THE DOOR OUT OF HELL

THE TITAN KISS

VOLCHIN
& OTHER STORIES

by

Clark Nida

Earthspot Books

Published by Earthspot Books, 2017
9 Normanby Terrace, Whitby, YO21 3ES, England.

Copyright © Clark Nida, 1964 - 2017.

The right of Clark Nida to be identified as author of this work has been asserted in accordance with Section 77 of the Copyright, Designs and Patents Act 1988.

No part of this publication may be reproduced, stored in a retrieval system, or transmitted in any form or by any means, electronic, mechanical, photocopying, recording or otherwise without the prior written consent of the publisher or a licence permitting copying in the UK issued by the Copyright Licensing Agency Ltd, 90 Tottenham Court Road, London W1P 9HE.

ISBN 978-1-898728-44-3

1 2 3 4 5 6 7 8 9

The following stories by the author writing under his real name (Ian Clark) first appeared as follows:

Volchin—Winning entry: NUF Short Story Competition, judged by Kingsley Amis.

Unit 5, New Universities Festival Issue, June 1966.

The Dark Before The Dawn—*Cum Grano 24*: Literary Magazine of the Students' Union, University of Keele. Summer Term, 1964.

A Hand in the Dark—1st Prize, Short Story Competition no.1, May 1992, *Weardale Gazette*, Bishop Auckland, DL13 2LA.

Don't Really Exist—*Bias*, vol. 2 no. 4, Festival 1965, University of Sussex.

The Katzendoppelgänger—*Your Cat*, Issue 5, Jan-Feb 1995, pp72-73, EMAP Publications (entitled "Haunted").

No Supper for Soddy—*Cum Grano 25*: Literary Magazine of the Students' Union, University of Keele. Autumn Term, 1964.

The following stories by the author writing as Clark Nida first appeared as follows:

Inner Space—*Murky Depths*, Issue #12, 2009.

We Don't Come From Round Here—A Song for the Bees: An anthology of stories, articles and poems by Whitby Writers. Ian Clark (ed). 2010. Undead Tree Publications, ISBN 978-1-898728-19-1 (Entitled "We Don't Come From Here").

Bad Star—*Murky Depths*, Issue #18, 2010.

FOREWORD

On retiring to Whitby, my father installed himself as a pillar of the local writers group, editing and producing numerous books and anthologies for his fellow authors, but after some years I noticed he still hadn't issued a collection of his own short stories, so with a cheek I knew he'd forgive, I quietly started producing *Volchin and Other Stories* to help make his short fiction accessible to friends and fans.

Compiling this volume has given me the pleasure of rediscovering these pieces and seeing them cohere into a substantial work that handsomely complements his science fiction novel *The Titan Kiss* and autobiographical novel *The Door Out of Hell.*

Naturally, any shortcomings in the editing or presentation in this volume are entirely mine.

Maxwell Clark
February 2017

CONTENTS

VOLCHIN

'The dog,' you will hear it pedantically asserted, 'was the first animal to be domesticated.'

There is an implicit rider to this: '…by man.' Over the last few thousand millennia, the dog, or rather the wolf, has had far more opportunity to domesticate… man. A wolf is as adaptable a creature as a man—with this difference. Men, *en masse*, tend to go in for pointless, wilful innovations when they have nothing better to do. Their gregarious instinct is that of cattle or chickens, setting up pecking orders and hierarchies. This reprehensible tendency results in those at the top being shielded from the fight for survival that is life by those at the bottom, permitting them to indulge their superfluous hobbies, their arts and sciences.

By contrast a wolf is adaptable, but it is not wilful. It tends to scorn pointless innovations. A shameless utilitarian, it must have the value of anything proven before acceptance, but then acceptance is without reservation. So when the bitch wolf loped home with a human baby carried in a maul caked with the blood of its parents, it wasn't because she was addicted to novelties. She had lost the last of her pups to a supercilious bird of prey and she needed something to suckle.

The baby had been discovered after the appetite of the pack had been sated, otherwise it would have made a tender snack in between manflesh and horseflesh. Its mother had pushed it into the snow under the sledge before her throat had been torn out. It was curiosity, not hunger, that had prompted the bitch to root out the bawling bundle.

Once it was obvious that the bitch was not going to be parted from it, her mate accepted it as part of the family. After all, the late-lamented pups had appeared, just like that, one day when he was out on the chase. It was twice the size of a six-week-old pup, but completely helpless and hairless. Apart from that there wasn't a surprising amount of difference to start with. Not until months later, when the winter was past and the conifers had stopped dripping, did it become apparent just how different the thing was.

It was not growing up.

It couldn't tear meat from the bone and needed it to be chewed. The bitch was still presenting it with her double row of black teats—with all that milk and meat surely it should begin to look less like an overgrown newborn pup? Don't be misled—the wolves knew all the time that their adopted pup was human and was not going to grow a shaggy coat. But humans were weird, dangerous animals—and yet this creature was so helpless!

With the warmer days the thing at last began to show traces of the peculiarities attributed to men. Although still no good at chewing, it actually had jaws on the ends of its forepaws, which it inserted into ears and mouths, pulled tails and fur and generally made itself uncomfortable to have to live with.

At no time did the wolves seriously consider getting rid of it. Certainly the bitch had landed the pair of them with something embarrassingly offbeat, but as with human mothers who have deformed children, there was a powerful instinct to protect the helpless changeling. The fact that the thing was showing a bit of life rather tended to encourage the foster-parents, but they had to suckle it through another white winter before it displayed much mobility.

The Old Wolf eyed its clumsy lumberings impatiently. It would trip and fall and emit a full rallying cry, and he'd have to go over and nuzzle it before it would quieten down. Quite of its own accord it used to rise on its hind legs and stretch out those peculiar forepaws to grasp leaves, stones and suchlike. The wolves weren't impressed. What was the point of delicate little prehensile pads that could carry only stones? They got hurt every time the thing tried to run. On balance they only seemed to have a negative value. Besides by now they should be teaching it to hunt, and all it could do was muck around with pebbles, which it even tried to eat on occasions.

Another litter of pups came. This made it easier for the pair to persevere with the baby, for they noticed with approval that it could certainly look after itself now, when it came to squabbling with its foster brothers over food. Whereas the pups had but one pair of jaws each, the thing had three, which it was beginning to use to great effect. Alas, it still couldn't run…

The running problem might never have been solved if wolves had trotted like most other quadrupeds. It so happens that wolves lope in much the same way with four legs as humans do with two, bringing both legs on the same side forward together. The baby's locomotion was still diagonal, true to humans' closer similarity to cattle than wolves, though he'd had occasion to mimic his foster-parents in everything else. On the frequent occasions that the Old Wolf had taken to harrying him in order to make him run however, he had tried to lope. This was a difficult operation with the hind legs growing distinctly longer than the forelegs, but gradually he evolved his own freestyle. With it he was able to cover significant distances at some semblance of speed without the delicate forepaws touching the ground. It was a gangling, flailing movement and when he stopped, gasping for breath, he dropped back on to all fours. The child literally learned to run before he could walk.

*　　*　　*

A full moon lit up the snow with a still gleam. The pine trees rising in a black bank further down the hill never moved—they might have been spiky outcrops of rock which the snow had spurned. On the hilltop grey snowy shapes were flitting all the time out of the forest. One lay back its ears and pointed its nose at the sky—its throat and chest an erect organ pipe that rang out the rallying howl over the black pine tops. The sound was copied in the distance, then again and again all around, as if rogue pines were howling amid their silent brethren. The snow yielded up more and more ghosts until they crept and flickered all over its moonlit expanse.

An unusual shape appeared out of the forest, but the wolves were not disturbed. It was a mascot of the pack they'd had around for as long as anyone could remember. It always put in an appearance when there was hunting to be done. For the most part they put up with it, although its sly ways could be irritating. Normally wolves not quite like the others did their hunting alone, or else they kept to the outskirts of the pack and picked over the leavings when the comrades had done with the pushing and shoving. They might find themselves eaten if they strayed into the thick of things. This mascot however could hold its own when compelled to. Its years of romping with wolves for playmates had taught it the canine weak points as well as its own, and the privileged treatment by a wolf family had led naturally to privileged treatment by the whole pack. Some of the bitches used to make up to it, and having apparently just made some discoveries attendant on this it was beginning actively to seek them out. It made with three or four—it seemed that one wasn't enough to keep the hairless creature warm at nights.

The leader was no doubt pondering all this when he saw the thing coming. He turned his whole enraged attention onto it. Perhaps the privileged treatment had been going on for too long; perhaps it was even a case of *cherchez la loupe*.

The leader's fangs gleamed brighter than the snow in his pine-black mouth. The slobbering hiss of insult was returned and the other wolves pulled back to watch, expressionless. There came a growl of surprise from the leader as the thing turned its back to stride to the edge of the forest. Coward!

The thing rapidly scratched in the snow for something, then reared on its hind legs as the wolf trotted over to meet it. As the pack converged for a good look, the antagonists snarled. Normally in a fight between two wolves on a point of honour one or the other would quickly capitulate before any real damage was done. The victor would never continue the violence, once satisfied with the submission and assured that all had seen it. But with no tail to put between its legs the changeling could not formally capitulate. So blood was about to flow.

The leader sprang. His head was seen to be deflected the moment before he crashed the thing to the ground. The two contestants rolled over in a struggling growling snowy mass and the pack crept closer. If they were in the habit of running a sweepstake the leader would have had the odds at that instant—which would have been a mistake, for his muzzle had just been shattered by a piece of flat rock. The combatants lay still as if asleep. At length the thing rose to its feet again and the wolf fell away quite limp.

Clenching its bloody fists and closing its eyes it howled, as the wolves dismantled their ex-leader.

Without much of a nose for the scent, the thing wouldn't have made a very good pack leader. Now its master, the venerable Old Wolf, stepped forward in his shaggy old age and demanded precedence. Again the unexpected—the thing seemed relieved to have the burden of initiative lifted from its shoulders and a brief nuzzle sealed an understanding that worked out surprisingly well. The Old Wolf was no match for any young dog that cared to challenge his authority, but a pretender would now face the prospect of taking on the pair of them together. Hardly fair on the younger generation.

But the Old Firm was so successful that the size of the pack grew and grew. One must not think of a wolf pack as a body with any official standing—it is merely an *ad-hoc* association for tackling the larger prey that is all that's available in winter time. Come summer and little animals creep out of their holes, the pack gives way to the family group for hunting. But now, in the depths of winter, the pack grew so large that it could even hunt the bear.

Here the wily human really got the chance to show what he could do, using a torn-off branch to push down a treed bear into the dancing jaws below. How he could climb trees not even he knew. From the wolves' point of view he should only have learned such a skill had he been taught by tree-climbing human parents. Of course the wolves couldn't be expected to know that human parents do not teach their children to climb trees. The children instinctively acquire this skill. Yet another example, if one were needed, of man's closer affinity with the most primitive mammals than with the far more advanced wolf.

But on the whole the wolves' tame man preferred to feel the ground under his feet and run down his quarry in open chase rather than pull it down from a tree. As was only right and proper.

The Old Wolf could now be proud of his adopted son. The man was certainly a good wolf to have on one's side.

*　　*　　*

It was the man's perverse love of novelty that proved his downfall. He took to closer and closer exploration of that area of the forest cleared and settled by humans—a thing that no wolf would ever do in the daytime unless desperate. If one came across humans, the thing to do was to look around for something else to hunt first. Unless one had at least a couple of dozen companions.

It wasn't as might be supposed that the thing was fascinated by their similarity in size and shape to himself—that wasn't so evident anyway until one had torn the outer covering off one of two. Everyone knows that a tame animal, like the wolves' tame human, is not really interested in the wild varieties of his own kind.

8

But the wild humans were very interested in him! They finally succeeded in capturing him too, but although they killed the Old Wolf and his other stout companions in the process, they were careful not to kill him, no matter how many of them he ripped at and slashed.

*   *   *

'*Mikula!*'

The surly peasant turned around from his sport of poking the cowering creature through the wooden bars of the cage.

'*Shto s'toboyu?*' he replied rudely, without first looking to see who had accosted him. Then he could only gape abashed before the black-cloaked newcomer. The other peasants shuffled backwards from the cage, caught in the act of tormenting a dumb creature.

For a moment the two gazed at each other through the lashed cage—the one with only his face uncovered, the other naked, covering his face with his fingers. The latter could recognise fear and loathing in any animal's eyes—he could see it in all the other eyes around him, now that they had stopped amusing themselves at his powerlessness.

But the black man's eyes were not like the others'. Indeed he stood regarding him in much the same way as the Old Wolf used to do, before harrying him in a despairing effort to teach him to run. The caged creature began to whimper. At that the black man

9

turned angrily upon his tormenters of late. What a funny gabbling noise these men made as they confronted each other. Perhaps they were going to fight? …No, definitely not. The black man had no difficulty asserting his superiority—but why was he carrying on snarling now that he had achieved his end?

When he stopped, the peasants moved forward once more, but this time they merely picked up the cage without trying to agitate its prisoner. The wolf-man quickly learned that by means of a protracted confrontation the black man could, on top of asserting his authority, make another perform a series of involved acts. This raised an interesting question: would he succeed in doing the same with him?

Just let him try!

*   *   *

They eventually found it safe to let him out of his cage.

For weeks these black men were the only animals he saw. They gave him food and he got quite used to them. But he pined for the pack, for the Old Wolf and for the crunch of dry snow under his feet. The only daylight he saw was a little brilliant square with bars across. He longed to get through that square, into the cold, bright open air, to chase a scampering buck and feel its warm furry throat quiver between his teeth, as limbs and lungs throbbed after the exertion.

He wasted away and didn't eat the food they brought him. Yes, he had tried to eat stones as a baby, but he couldn't eat the hot fibrous mush they laid before him. When he fell sick—which was the first opportunity to take him from the cage—only then did they give him raw meat, which he ate voraciously. But they brought it sparingly and with evident distaste.

The abbot appeared and wafted towards the wild creature lying miserably in the corner, wrapped in skins. As he squatted down, the creature cringed away. He spoke to him: complex sounds, quite without significance. But his listener couldn't help noticing that this murmuring was not reflex action of the mandibles, nor stomach noises, but entirely voluntary and therefore done for his benefit. What did it signify? Why was the man making those peculiar moans and hisses and clicks?

Gradually a pattern became apparent. A definite pattern of sounds was being repeated at different speeds, but usually slowly, so as to display every facet of this intricate oral activity.

At length the man got up and went away. But he came back the next day, and the day after. He kept on coming back. In the long solitude of illness the creature took to mimicking some of the curious new sounds he was hearing. But when the abbot appeared, he kept silent.

Here was a strange thing. The humans would make these noises to each other and invariably something happened. Now for the first time they were being directed at him—and nothing happened! He guessed that were he to respond, something would certainly happen—but how was he to know it wouldn't be something unpleasant?

The abbot came again, as he always did. The creature now no longer cringed away from him and, what was more, the urge to lunge was passing with the very sickness that had made it impossible.

'*Ya—Piotr,*' said the man in black. '*Ya—Piotr. Ya—Piotr.*'

In spite of himself he murmured '*ya…*' very quietly.

Something did happen! Instantly the man sprang out of his serenity. He caught hold of his hands as if to present the sounds to him irresistibly. '*Piotr! Piotr! Gavaree: Piotr!*'

'*Piotr…*'

The result wasn't unpleasant, only somewhat frightening. These humans nuzzled a bit like wolves. The abbot wasn't finished yet, though. He assayed further, emitting the rest of the now familiar sequence of sounds.

'*…Ah tuy—Volchin!*' The man pointed his forefinger at him.

'*Volchin…*' the creature repeated more confidently.

'*Da, Volchin! Volchin! Tuy ponimayesh!… Volchin!*'

The man in black got up and rushed from the room. His voice could be heard loudly addressing the others of his kind, who answered with cries of surprise. What was happening? Were they panicking? The creature waited apprehensively, wondering what they

were going to do next. He didn't have long to wait—
the abbot reappeared with a large piece of red meat.

*　*　*

It was only much later that he learned that his name,
Volchin, referred to the *volki*, or wolves, from whence
he came to the monastery. At the time it was a totally
abstruse concept to grasp—that of having a name—to
which he only contrived via the inducement of red
meat. Do not deprecate him for that. There are saints
who have attained the highest truths for much baser
reasons. Wolves don't have names, nor have they the
slightest use for them. One's scent is one's identity.
Why humans should disregard this simple, efficient
convention for the over-sophisticated one of assigning
an intricate noise to each individual on a completely
arbitrary basis was inexplicable. On its own merits it
would have been pointless to concern oneself with it.
But there was red meat involved—and that was
sufficient justification for a wolf.

*　*　*

Three years later he could converse so well that his
breeding might have been ordinary peasant stock.
Though to say that does the wolves scant justice. The
monk Volchin grew in favour with his brethren and his
superiors as time passed. He distinguished himself not

13

only by his holiness and dedication, applying himself to the work in hand with dog-like obedience, but also by his ability to fast for long periods and to run tirelessly on errands over prodigious distances. Wolfish necessities, but saintly virtues to these austere pioneering monks.

The monastery had until recently been an outpost deep in the forest, founded by a few devout monks who preferred the harsh discipline of the wild to a soft life in the established mother house. In its turn it too had become 'established' of late, acquiring a halo of farms and peasant villages to cushion it from the oppressive proximity of the woods. Oppressive, that is, to the newcomer from Moscow—no longer the proud frontier city founded by the Varangian Swede, Yuri of the Long Arm, but of late the most trusted handmaid of the Golden Horde ('Health to our Eastern Masters!').

Abbot Piotr, Volchin's superior, was a founder member of the monastery and rued the success of this pioneering venture. He yearned for the old days, when life really was life—not the sluggish ease of fasting with a larder full of the tithes of peasants. Fasting when you know that an empty larder awaits the end of your formal penance is real fasting. Volchin couldn't agree more—who could possibly think otherwise?

It seemed that only the hard core of founder members thought this way. They didn't make a fuss about it. One day they just nodded to each other, there was a sending for subordinates by spiritual directors, and the next day they left.

'Seventy versts to the East!' Piotr had exclaimed to Volchin in rapture. And Volchin's eyes had gleamed with the gleam of moonlight on the snowy hillside.

After they had departed, the new abbot, a Muscovite, was heard to remark 'it was well that they took the wolf-man with them, rather than to have left him here with us.' Only newly acquainted with Volchin, he was nonetheless relieved to think that he would never be seeing him again.

However he did see him again. Two weeks later a peasant came running up to Abbot Ilya in the fields.

'They have caught the wolf-man and are beating him,' he gasped. 'He says that the company of holy monks are all dead!'

As the Muscovite strode quickly to the eastern gate, he saw a knot of peasants flailing staves. They stopped at his approach. They would not have dared to touch Volchin had he been wearing his habit.

'Volchin,' cried the abbot to the wretch. 'Why have you returned?'

'Holy Piotr—Sviatoslav—all the company—dead! Wolves killed them.'

'You betrayed them to the wolves!' screamed a peasant, lashing him across the face. 'You are a Judas!'

Volchin looked appealingly towards the abbot. The Muscovite turned away in revulsion.

*　　*　　*

An hour later Volchin was lying face downwards in the cool wet mud. It was many years since he'd tasted human blood. His aching, pounding body was cooling slowly in sweat and his heart, writhing inside his chest, was writhing just that bit slower than it did when he first stopped running.

Now that Piotr was dead, human beings had become strange wild animals once more. What an age away it seemed, since he was at Piotr's side—with wolves squatting or lying down some thirty yards away. They waited like the besiegers of Jerusalem.

'Go back and tell Ilya what has happened to us. Could you get past all those wolves? If any one of us can—you can!'

'I cannot leave you, Piotr.'

'You cannot disobey. Ilya must know. You must tell him everything—how we took your advice lightly—how you were right after all.'

But instead of listening to him, these erstwhile friendly men had tried to beat him to death. Once more they had treated him like they did all wolves. To whom now could he turn? There was nobody, absolutely nobody. He might just as well have stayed to die under the peasants' sticks.

He raised his head. There, straight in front of him, a young wolf and an old wolf stood watching.

The young wolf was glancing at the old wolf from time to time. He was taking his cue from him, but wondering why his vastly more experienced companion hung back from perfectly good prey—a solitary wounded man. But the older wolf just stood and stared.

Wolf and man regarded each other for a long while with the selfsame gaze. The old wolf crept round and Volchin crept round too, spiralling closer. The young wolf squatted down to watch, completely at a loss. The point that he just couldn't grasp, naturally enough, was that these two recognised each other!

Except that now Volchin smelt of humans, too— no longer the mascot-champion of that legendary pack in this ancient wolf's prime. But these territorial memories linger about wolves with their own body smells. Two wolves might sniff each other and one would wag his tail as if to say 'so you used to knock about with the 'Lads' too, eh?'

At this juncture Volchin realised that it was going to be the same old problem with him as it had always been—no tail to wag.

The old wolf's tail clung tightly to the backs of his heels. His jaws parted and he sighed quietly.

Straightaway the young wolf jumped up and lunged. A quick flurry and it was all over.

Of course the wolves did the right thing. Suppose you owned a working sheepdog and the creature 'went wild'. Anyone who came across it again would be required to destroy it. One simply cannot afford to be soft-hearted.

THE DARK BEFORE THE DAWN

'If I hadn't got up to check the gas was turned off, what would I be doing now? Well, not all that different, but it would be in a nice comfortable bed. So what? It's not at all bad here. Besides, I've never spent the night in a kitchen. There's always a first time, they say. And I can see the window from here, too…

'The sky is a dark glowing grey and a single star is beaming down into my little kitchen. My children used to tell me the stars were thousands of miles away. Unbelievable! For although I cannot read a magazine these days, I can still see a thousand miles.

'How much I still have!

'My children have all left me now. Bill—dear Billy—lost in the War. Margaret's in America, having a good time. Peter… I haven't heard from him for years now. Please God that he's still happy. I know he must be. Surely he'd have written to me if he was in trouble.

'Life is funny. You bring children into the world, care for them, dry their tears when they fall over… and now there's nobody left to pick you up when you're down yourself.'

*　*　*

She could recognise various things about her, but she'd never seen them from this angle before. Straight ahead was indefinite blackness. Her star vanished when she gazed directly at it, but lit up bright as ever when she shifted her gaze. Everything was visible all around her in various shades of ghostly grey. Intangible gas stove and shelves which disappeared every now and then in a spasm of straining to see.

How alert she was! And how loudly that clock had started ticking. Never mind. It wouldn't keep her awake. It couldn't—nothing could. She felt so warm and cosy. So comfy and sleepy.

'How lucky I am! And to think what a job I had trying to get to sleep last night. Now Mabel will come in the morning and pick me up, and she'll make a cup of tea, and we'll have a little chat...'

*　*　*

The parish priest, inoffensive, nice little man, fingered his cards nervously. He was trying to catch her eye. Mabel next to her said 'Two hearts', but this was rather silly because she had nearly all the hearts in her own hand.

Moloch, sitting opposite Mabel, sniggered obscenely. 'Have you noticed,' he said in his sneering voice, 'how rarely one finds true lovers together? One may love, but how often is that love returned?'

He leered sideways at her and cuddled his cards to himself, gloating. A repulsive young man. He smelt of sulphur and cheap brilliantine and reminded her of someone she didn't like.

It was Father O'Reilly's turn. 'Two spades.'

'Ah,' said Moloch. 'You've come to bury us, not to praise!'

The allusion was lost on poor, shrinking Father O'Reilly, who had only just come over from a very uneducated part of Ireland.

'My turn,' chuckled Moloch. 'I'll go five coshes.'

'Five hearts,' she breathed defiantly at the young fellow. His upper lip curled and he seemed to coil back inwardly for a sarcastic riposte of unbearable scorn.

'Six clubs,' Mabel interposed quickly, though obviously dismayed at her partner's bid.

The poor little priest was getting very agitated. He looked pitifully up at her, his eyebrows framing a desperate, hopeless question. Poor Father O'Reilly. He was so ready to help people, but he obviously couldn't give them what he had not got himself. It wasn't surprising that he didn't have the heart to go on.

And Moloch knew it—the swine! This was clear from what he'd said. Now he looked with brazen contempt at the cringing little Irishman as he mumbled something about hearts, then he leaned back in his chair and barked with derision. His eyes, loaded with ersatz charm, were now levelled at her as he said meaningfully, 'I pass'…

*　　*　　*

The clock ticked away on the mantelpiece and the silent star shone steadily in the four-square pane of luminous grey. She blinked and took a deep breath and as she did so her lower abdomen ached warningly. It had become hard and uncomfortable all of a sudden. Her back was aching and other regions felt numb.

'I wonder if I dare turn over. I'd be much more comfortable on my side...

'Oh!' A vicious flaming pain scorched up from her lower abdomen as she stirred slightly and she collapsed back with a gasp. She had to screw her face up while the pain slowly drained away to a bearable level. Oh, but it was horrible!

'So that's that. I'll just have to stay like this till morning.' And she tried to compose herself and settle down to the long hours of waiting... tick... tick... tick... tick... on... and on... and on...

'I wonder what the time is.'

She couldn't see the clock from there, only hear it.

That does it! Tomorrow she'd ask Mabel if she knew anyone who had a chiming clock. They're quite out of fashion nowadays. Surely they'd exchange it for a kitchen clock. It's old, but it goes very well when it's on its back. She wouldn't really miss it... But with a chiming clock you'd have to remember to wind up the chimes. She'd get Mabel to do that.

A chiming clock. How nice...

*　*　*

'Bill! You're here! You're back!'

He was standing there beside her, right beside her, looking down into her eyes. But sadly… oh so sadly. She remembered how he used to look as a little boy when he was just about to burst into tears. He looked like that now.

'Yes, Mother, I'm back.'

'My, whatever's the matter? Have you lost something?'

He looked distracted and didn't seem to hear the question. 'Why are you lying down there on the floor, Mother?'

'Oh, Bill, I am glad to see you. Now please—be an angel and help me up. Oh, you always were such a good boy to your old mother. Your brother and sister have gone off and left me all on my own, you know. Did I tell you?'

'No, Mother.'

'Didn't you hear me? Not in my prayers?'

'Prayers…' His voice seemed far off.

'Bill, my love…!'

He knelt down beside her and gently stroked her forehead. 'Yes, Mother, you're all right now. You're all right! Don't worry anymore. Not now.'

'Billy, Billy,' and her eyes brimmed over. 'Don't leave me, please Billy… never again… Billy…'

…Tick… tick… tick… The clock intruded upon her consciousness. What's the matter with it? Had it stopped…?

'My God,' she choked. 'I'm seeing things. I
thought —'

A blank disappointment settled upon her like a
shroud. 'And yet it—it seemed so natural! It just didn't
occur to me… I forgot he's dead.'

She found she was shivering and she suddenly felt
a spasm of cold, like a bucket of filthy water sloshed
over her lungs and entrails.

'I'm going delirious. I'm not going to last the
night.'

The utter hopelessness of the situation opened to
her like a door. She felt the bitter, soothing draught of
despair, wafting the veil from something in her. Mabel
wasn't coming in the morning, she remembered now.
How silly of her to hope for it. But it wouldn't have
mattered anyway, even if she had been. She recalled
what happened to old Mrs Birdall. She was dead in the
morning when they found her.

A sudden impulse and she called out. Her voice
deafened her, echoing inside her skull. 'Help! Help!
Oh…!' She tailed off as her broken pelvis exploded
with pain.

*   *   *

The clock ticked on. Not a sound apart from that.
There was nobody around. Nobody else was awake in
the whole wide world and no one could be woken,
either. She tried a little croak of self-pity and realised

that her shouting hadn't been much louder than that. Just a mournful wail.

Her sight grew dim. She barely noticed the silhouette that appeared outside the partly-open window. It took a moment, then it registered… and a rich flood of relief surged through her body. It was Hector!

With a hiss of scraping fur Hector slid through, regaining his feline shape with a tail-erecting flourish. He was here—her saviour! Her only friend in the world now, come in the time of her direst need.

'Come here, Hector,' she murmured painfully and made a little sucking noise with her wrinkled lips.

Plonk. He landed on the floor forepaws first and a moment later there was his pointed nose nuzzling into her ear in jerky little sniffs. Her arm sluggishly felt for him and fondled the soft warm fur. Hector purred and curled up by her cheek.

'Dear Hector,' she moaned. 'Dear, dear Hector.' And she felt she was being lulled by waves and gently rocked under a tropical sky…

It had never been dark night. She had been here all afternoon, lying in the bottom of the pea-green boat, warmed through by the sun, with Hector by her side.

'Where are we going, Hector?'

'Far away. I'm taking you away from all that. We're going to a desert island where we can live out the rest of our days in carefree abandon.'

'Oh, Hector!'

'No need to stint yourself for me anymore,' he waved his black hand. 'No more saving for my food out of your pension. There's fish in the lagoon and acres of coconuts filled with milk. No more Kit-E-Kat for me, or for you—we're in the lap of luxury!'

'Hector, how clever of you to think of all this.'

'Not at all. Nothing is too good for you, oh Mistress-mine. The slightest qualm, the slightest discomfort… anything the matter?'

'My head. I—I'm afraid the rocking and bobbing is making me dizzy. I think I'm going to be seasick…'

'Let's go back,' Hector murmured in her ear.

*   *   *

There she was, back in her darkened kitchen. She felt for Hector but he wasn't there anymore.

'Life is funny,' she said aloud in a croak. She carried on in her mind because it was too much effort to speak. 'You bring up cats, feed them, care for them—and when you're down, they go away and leave you in the lurch.'

The nausea which ended her dream came back in a rush. She nearly vomited, but it sank back, leaving intense cold in its place.

She was an icicle, hanging in a forest of gleaming white needles.

Now she was rattling and slithering round a tumbler and whisky was being sloshed over her. It burned through her skin and set fire to her stomach.

Then it went out and she cooled down again. Something icy scuttled across her forehead. It was a bead of sweat.

Cold… cold… cold…

Bright, white cold. She puffed a cloud of breath, a dense, white, palpitating cauliflower that floated upwards for a long time before it dispersed. But the passengers sitting opposite her made never a move— they just stared back frigidly.

She bounced up and down on her seat restively, impulsively, and examined her colourful knitted mittens. Ticktockticktockticktock went the wheels of the train as they scampered across the icy rails—and she was tickled to see that the gentleman in the corner had icicles in his beard! In fact all the passengers seemed to have a good coating of hoar frost except herself, young, vivacious and warm-blooded.

The cold air burned her cheeks but it didn't make them numb. But oh!—her fingers! She wanted to throttle a few of her fellow passengers, just to give her fingers some exercise. The temptation was getting far too strong, so all of a sudden she got up and thrust her way out of the compartment.

The powdery snow was an inch deep in the corridor. The only other person there was a man, stamping his feet and panting every so often. She couldn't help staring at him. He had no frost on him at all!

He in his turn stopped, cocked his head on one side and gave her an enigmatic look. Quizzical?

Playful? She recognised his face, but couldn't place him.

'Why are all those people in there covered in frost?'

'Because, my pretty young nineteen-year-old, they are cold,' he replied. 'Inside and out.'

Of course. It was her husband. How young he looked!

'When did this train journey start?'

'Oh, years and years ago,' he answered blandly. 'They were born frozen and they were brought up like it.'

'But when is it going to end?'

'Is it?' (He did have an exasperating way with people sometimes.)

'Oh, don't kid me! Of course it is.'

'Well, if you say so…'

He laughed. She went up and took hold of his warm lapels. 'I want to get off!'

He replied soothingly, 'You will, my dear, very soon. Follow me at the next station, just before we get to the Dawn…'

*　　*　　*

It was now pitch-black in the kitchen and she was meeting her body head-on in deadly battle, setting her toothless jaw against the magnetic pull of her pelvis, which was poisoning her system into numbness. No! It was not going to reach her brain. She was determined

not to drop off. She was going to stay awake, under
pain of death.

Ah, she knew what had happened now. She had
had a blackout and fallen. Old people's bones are
weak. It was a stroke. Of course it was. The pulsing in
her head—the nausea. Were the pelvis and the brain
conspiring to kill her? She wouldn't stand for it.

'No, Paul. I'm not going to follow you. Not yet!'

Not to fall asleep, under pain of death. But what a
fight! She began muttering to keep awake and to shake
her head to and fro. Yes, she was shaking it off. She
was winning!

'Oh Mabel, come soon! I can't hold out for
ever…'

It's Always Darkest Just Before The Dawn. The
words formed themselves into a shape. It had a
hopeful, mauve sort of colour.

With a thrill she noticed the sky outside the
window. Black cloud had swept away her star, but a
rent in the cloud revealed a lighter sky behind. Not the
intense glow of dark night, but a real colour you could
actually *see* when looking straight at it.

She was home! The Dawn…

*   *   *

Mabel unlocked the door. 'Cooee, Mrs D. Are you
about?'

'…Oh!' She rushed into the kitchen and knelt down beside the old lady. 'Ow, Mrs D! What happened? Are you—?'

A BEER TOO MANY

Apart from the units of account being loaves of bread and jugs of beer, a papyrus from the thirteenth pharaonic dynasty (c. 1600 BCE)[1] is surprisingly consistent with present-day accounting practice. There is, however, a remarkable error in the beer column: the figures don't add up but the columns are balanced as if they did. That's not unknown in present-day accounting practice either.

'What have you brought that home for? Haven't we got enough of it in the house already?'

'Don't be deceived by appearances, Tabubu, my love. What is standing before your eyes is our ruin.'

The porter had deposited a coarse brown jug on their beautiful rush mat, a tessellated Joseph's coat of greens and blues. He bowed and silently withdrew. Scribe Nebankh threw himself into his carved ebony chair as if he had himself been dumped from the back of the porter's invisible twin.

His wife regarded him with indifference. Every evening he drooped home like a spent ass laden with the cares of the world. He never listened to her day. He was forever wrapped up in himself and his own miseries.

---

[1] Gardiner, 1957

'I don't call a jug of beer ruin,' she said brightly. 'Let me send for Inni to broach it for you and bring you a drinking reed.'

'N-no, not that one!' He struggled forward feebly with his arm outstretched towards the jug, then flopped back with a sigh. 'I don't want a beer. I don't feel I could manage one. I must think… think!' He clawed at his face.

Tabubu suddenly felt a pang of concern. Rising from her cushions, she snatched up a lotus from the bowl and stroked his forehead whilst holding the flower to his nostrils.

'What is the matter, my brother, my love? Relax in my shadow. Rinse out your heart.'

Nebankh stretched as if in agony. 'Tomorrow I shall come home with stripes on my back. If I come home at all and don't find myself on a one-way trip to the Paths of Horus. And all because of this jug of beer.'

'The Paths of Horus? Is it really as bad as that?' She chuckled. 'I can't see you lasting very long in Fortress Zero.'

'Go on, laugh at me. Shrivel my *ka* with your mirth. How you'll laugh when you go down to the riverbank as a poor washerwoman. How our children will laugh as they beg in the streets.'

'My Dear Heart! What can have befallen you? Tell me all.'

With eyes closed Nebankh lolled his head from
side to side beneath his wife's caresses. 'Sobekiry...' he
began.

Her hands dropped to her side. 'I might have
known,' she said. 'What has he done now?'

She didn't wait for him to answer. Something
made her realise the seriousness of what had
happened. Turning, she clapped for her handmaid,
who came scurrying in from the boudoir. Together
they lifted Nebankh's feet onto the footstool and took
off his gilded straw sandals. The maid fetched a
decanter of wine, from which Tabubu poured a dash
into her husband's cup.

'Oh cunning Thoth, who taught mankind to read,'
he muttered, 'Give me the understanding to read aright
what I see.'

As if the effort was more than he could manage he
swirled the cup three times widdershins and then cast
the gobbet of wine into the brazier. Up it went—
poosh!—in a cloud of spirity steam. Both he and his
wife huddled over the cup, peering at the flecks of
sediment, then Nebankh slumped back with a groan.

Without a word Tabubu refilled the cup from the
flask, this time pouring the wine through a strainer. As
he drank it, she said 'You know your trouble? You're
too soft-hearted. You should have got rid of that rascal
long ago.'

'I'm just waiting for my opportunity to catch him
out. Likewise he watches and waits for me to make a
mistake. He's done so ever since I had his brother

stretched out for petty pilfering. But at last he's got me. I can't see any way out of it. Tomorrow he'll denounce me to Number One.'

'You haven't really been fiddling, have you?'

'Of course not. Would I be so stupid?'

Tabubu didn't answer.

*　*　*

That night Nebankh lay awake, sweating in spite of the cold. Twice Tabubu had rolled over, taking the linen coverlet with her. Three times his ivory headrest had tipped over, giving him a sharp jab in the neck. Unable to lie still any longer, he crept quietly out of bed, taking care not to disturb his snoring wife.

Moonlight leaked down from the clerestory windows onto the parlour floor, glinting off the jug of beer. In the ghostly light it reminded him of the four canopic urns he had placed with his own hands in his mother-in-law's tomb. A funereal jug of guts, come back to haunt him. Skirting it widely, he crossed the mat to his writing chest and rummaged in the shadows among his scrolls. He took out a tiny tract he had purchased on impulse in the market one day. On the outside it said 'Effective Charm against a Nightmare'. Breaking the seal he unrolled it.

Take a loaf of bread and a jug of beer.
Eat some of the bread and drink some of the beer.
Meanwhile recite the following spell:

34

He uttered an obscenity and dropped the scroll into
the brazier. A few ashes still glowed dimly at the
bottom and a pungency, like incense, arose to his
nostrils. For a moment his heart was lifted, but
cynicism supervened. All these papyri were fit for was
to burn on coals to make a nice smell, he considered.
No doubt that was how they'd all end up.

He slid the bolts and opened the front door. The
lower pivot grated as it turned in its socket. Normally
he would have called Inni, whatever the time of day or
night, to put some tallow down to lubricate it. But now
he simply shrugged. Someone else's problem.

He strolled out onto the moonlit porch between
the two columns of *meru* wood, painted and gilded to
represent bundles of papyrus reeds in bloom. Once
long ago, he recalled, in the days of Imhotep and
Hordedef, great houses really did have bundles of
reeds as columns. But wood was so much more
durable. Expensive though it was, since it all had to be
imported from Byblos, everyone had wooden pillars.
His own were particularly fine, a prime feature of this
desirable residence. He wondered who would enjoy
them in days to come.

Around his pool the sycamores susurrated in the
dark breeze. All else was stillness apart from the small
ticking things of the night. Frogs belched from the
lotus pads on the black waters and the moon
shimmered in reflection.

He went to the pool's edge and knelt down. Ever so slowly he lowered his lips to the water surface. It was a delicious thing to do in the heat of the day, but now, in the chill of night, it was the kiss of the grave.

'I shall go down to my everlasting house…' he quoted quietly. But would his body ever rest in the tomb he had so painstakingly prepared for himself? In disgrace, nobody enjoys the *hotep di nsw*, the king's pension in perpetuity. Like Osiris, his body would thrown in the Nile. Down he would go to chat up the fishes, as the song went, to say hello to the phagrus and the loach.

And would Tabubu scour the seas, like Isis, looking for his body, to encase it in cedar wood and make it good for all eternity? Would she indeed! She was a good wife, as northern women go, but he had no illusions of her loyalty to him in disgrace.

There was one way out. If he were to die tonight he would rob Sobekiry of his victory. A dead man cannot be called upon to stand before the Thirty Councillors. The Ten Books could not be opened to accuse one who was lying prone in the House of Beauty. His *ka* would be suffered to live on, bathed in the perpetual light of sunrise, forever beholding the face of Ra.

The thought of his *ka* struck him with sudden force. Wait a minute! He couldn't possibly die tonight—his tomb wasn't in a fit state to receive him yet. What was to be done?

He made feverish plans. Tomorrow at the first
hour he would cross the river to the western bank.
Anpur would be there by the time he arrived, getting
down to work on the decor. At least he'd better be, or
he'd change his undertaker—yet again. Then he
remembered that it was too late to do that. Anyway,
once assured that everything was in order, or had a
chance of being so at the end of the regulation seventy
days' embalming, he could come back, go to bed and
breath out his *ba* in peace.

> *For He That has Gone to the Other Side*
> *Is as One who exults as a Living God*
> *Dispensing punishment upon the evildoer.*

Shuddering in the chill dark he turned to go back
inside. Moving purposefully, now that he was set on a
course of action, he crept silently into the pantry. A
quick check revealed enough powdered mandrake to
fell an ox. Whatever did Tabubu need it all for? Never
mind. Mixed with wine it would do the trick.

> *For He That has Gone to the Other Side*
> *Is One Who stands in the Bark of the Sun,*
> *Endowing the temples with the pick of the Land.*

A little wine now wasn't a bad idea. It would warm
him up and he might sleep when he went back to bed.
He didn't trouble with libations to Thoth this time, nor
did he fiddle about with flask and strainer. Instead he
took a swig straight from the bottle, knowing that it
would stir up the lees and make it undrinkable for
days. What did that matter now? He inserted the

pointed bottom of the bottle back into its wicker
stand, gingerly for fear of waking somebody with its
scratching sound.

> *For He That has Gone to the Other Side*
> *Is a Man of Sapience, whom none can gainsay,*
> *Whose every word is a Prayer to God.*

Selecting a loaf in the form of two upraised arms he bit
off the right hand. He always did that as a child. His
mother would scold him as he was apt to waste the
arms.

'Eat it all,' she would say. 'It's good for your *ka*. '

Don't we spend our entire lives doing what's good
for our *ka*? he thought. Wouldn't it be lovely to be like
a sand trotter and forget all about your *ka*. Pretend you
hadn't got one. Smear your body with resin and chew
garlic. Huff bad breath in people's faces and shrivel
their *ka* to cocoa pods. You could have a lot of fun in
life if you didn't have to bother about your *ka*—the
oh-so-fragile *ka*—immortal, but not imperishable.

He threw away the butt of the tiny loaf and
searched around for some raisins.

And yet... and yet you ought to worry. Life was so
transient. Nothing of yesterday's pleasure ever
remained to soften the pains of today. It was all
wasted, all those lotus flowers strewn about the dinner
table. All those cones of scented grease trickling down
your cheeks as you watched the dancing girls twirl and
prance. What remains? Silence and shadows, dust and
decay. You might as well have never been born.

Taking the lid of a small basket he was pleased to discover a pile of dates. If he couldn't have raisins, then he would eat dates. All of them. Who cared about indigestion? It was something safely in the future.

Yet once your body was reduced to a sticky black shell, swaddled and lacquered and laid in a box, something might remain. Something that might last for millions of years, until Osiris comes again to revive the dying world and make it send forth green shoots. Provided the king's endowment did not fail and your name stayed on the lips of the living, provided your enemies left you alone, the poor didn't raid your tomb, carry you off and throw you out onto the uplands, Osiris might find something left of you to make anew. It was for this slim hope of eternal life in some symbolic world that you scraped and saved, spending more on your tomb than you did on your house, building in rock instead of mud, with pillars of stone instead of timber.

All these hopes were dashed by disgrace. A man's eternal life could be ruined by the stroke of a pen. The sheer pointlessness of it all. He spat another date stone onto the floor.

*　　*　　*

He could see Sobekiry leering at him now. The pair of them were sitting opposite each other, checking the papyrus dockets which registered the flow of goods into and out of the storeroom.

39

'Two hundred loaves from yesterday,' said Sobekiry, 'all distributed. Two hundred fresh loaves to be carried over to tomorrow.'

'Correct. But the bread's not in question. It all adds up and we both agree. The word of two against none—case dismissed. It's the beer that's the problem.'

'Too right. Well, let's go down the list once more, this time very carefully.'

'Very well. I'll just read out the beer column. Amount of revenue of the Lord (Life, Wealth, Health!), Year 3, Month 2 of the Inundation, last day: 135 jugs of beer.'

'Correct.'

'Income as King's Portion from the Temple of Amun: 10 jugs.'

'Correct.'

'Now for the expenditure. To the Palace, against the signature of Butler of the Harim: 45 jugs.'

'Correct.'

'Storehouse ration to the Nurses' Quarters: 61 jugs.'

'Correct.'

'Storehouse ration to the Commoners of the Household: 38 jugs.'

'Correct.'

'You tot all that up and the balance is: one jug of beer. That's what it would have come to when I was at school. Don't you agree with that?'

'But I see two jugs of beer, not one.'

'Yes, but admit it. The figures say one jug.'

'I'm not admitting anything. You're the Scribe of Accounts, Nebankh. I'm only the checker. It's up to you to put things right.'

Nebankh had opened his mouth to protest, but Sobekiry had him cold. To ask to compare figures was to invite collusion, in front of witnesses too. The porters were still sitting there, watching the two scribes with fascination. Nebankh had tried to send them away but Sobekiry bade them stay, since there might be questions to answer. They needed no prompting, for they were itching to see the outcome of this altercation. They had never known anything like it. Usually the discrepancy was the other way, in which case they would have been only too glad to push off.

'Look, it's not as if there's anything missing. We've had that situation before. We simply have the porters stretched out until one of them owns up to having pilfered it. But instead there's a jug over. Surely we can resolve that with the greatest of ease?'

'How do you propose to do that?' said Sobekiry cunningly.

The instant he'd spoken, Nebankh knew he had said the wrong thing. The porters were wriggling with delight. They had sat there like wise monkeys with their hands over their mouths, nominally out of respect for their superiors, but really to hide the grins on their silly faces.

'Look, let's not make a pyramid out of a mud pile,' Nebankh had said. He winced to remember how badly he had underestimated the gravity of the situation even then. 'Let's both get up and take a stroll in the palace gardens. If we both pray hard to the Lord of Khemenu I wouldn't be surprised if the problem didn't sort itself out by the time we got back.'

He had glanced at the two porters as he said this, expecting to see a hint of approval in their faces. But their eyes were veiled. If they had known in good time how things were, they'd have had no difficulty in furnishing the solution themselves. But, as it happened, this was better by far—to sit and listen to these two learned scribes squabbling over a seemingly intractable problem.

Sobekiry shook his head slowly. 'Scribe Nebankh, I'm ashamed of you. Have you no fear of the Council? Would you not tremble to think that this might come to the ears of our gracious Lord?—Life, Wealth and Health be unto Him!'

'But it's only a spare jug of beer!'

'So you say. You'll be telling me next it's only an arithmetical error. But that's the whole reason you're sitting here and not plying an oar on the river—to get the figures right. If word came to Number One about this, would he dismiss it as no more than a tiny cone of dressed alabaster, sticking out of the desert sands? Might he not wonder what would be revealed if the sands were cleared away?'

Nebankh had swallowed painfully. Whatever he did, he must not let the porters see his discomfiture.

'What do you suggest we do about it?' he had asked, as innocently as he could.

'What do I suggest? Is this the wise Nebankh speaking—at whose behest people have been disgraced and beaten for similar discrepancies? I would not dare to suggest a thing. It is for you to get yourself out of the hole you're in.'

'In days to come, I shall recall your refusal to cooperate.'

Sobekiry had leaned forward, the flame of spite in his eyes. 'I'd rather have it so, than be accused along with you of pilfering one single jug of Pharaoh's beer. If the figures are wrong, you do not deserve your position. If the figures are right, then someone has not got their ration. It's no good asking them. They'll all swear on their heads they're short. But tomorrow— mark my words—someone will be back, full of accusations. They will not believe that the learned Nebankh was unaware that he had misdirected their jug of beer. He, at whose slightest word the stars themselves stoop to listen.' Sobekiry had stood up. 'Well, I'm off to make my report.'

Nebankh didn't doubt that he was off to make mischief. What would he try to do? If Sobekiry's statement of accounts showed a balance of two jugs, then woe betide Nebankh if two jugs did not go back into store. If, like his own, Sobekiry's balance showed one jug, then it would be fatal to send two jugs back into store, because one of them would never get there and nobody would ever say where it went. The jug doubtless belonged to somebody, who might well complain. Anyway, if Sobekiry wanted to, he would denounce Nebankh for deliberately losing an allegedly surplus jug, and there'd be witnesses to that, too.

His mind had been in a whirl. What should he do? He gave orders for one jug to be taken back to the storehouse. Then he commanded one of the porters to carry the spare jug home with him. That way he could keep an eye on it until its fate was determined.

It was only on the way home that he had realised that, whatever he did, he was trapped. Now he had given Sobekiry the opportunity to accuse him of having misappropriated it for his own use. Once more the porters were witnesses to that.

*   *   *

At first light he was grateful to get out of bed. Still he had not slept—no more than a fitful dream, perhaps. It might have told him something, but he couldn't remember what it was all about. Wandering around the house with a sickly feeling in the pit of his stomach he almost fell over his son Pepi, crouching in a doorway.

'I'm watching these ants fighting', the boy explained.

Normally he'd have asked who was winning, our side or theirs, but today he was overwhelmed by the thought that he was looking upon his only son for the last time. Placing his hands upon the boy's head, shaven except for a single plait at the side, he said:

44

'Pepi, my Son. My Avenger. Will you promise me something?'

'What?' said the boy, wondering if this was the prelude to some ingenious telling off.

'Will you come and pour water for me when I go down into the west?'

'When? Today?'

'In seventy days' time.'

This was too much for Pepi to take in. Unable to say so in words, he gazed appealingly at his father to explain himself.

'I'm afraid our Lord's grace is running out for us, Pepi. I'm sure you'd prefer to have a dead man of honour as your father than one alive, but disgraced. Whatever happens, remember how fond I was of you. Remember what good times we had together, picking cornflowers in our fields… hunting ducks in the marshes…'

A little frown creased the bridge of Pepi's snub nose. Still he said nothing. Nebankh drew his head forward and kissed his forehead.

'Never mind, Pepi. Now run along and find Miriammon for me. Tell her I have an important errand for her.'

Pepi got to his feet and sped off. As he ran he thought, 'A disgraced father. His *ka* all in pieces. Whatever will they say at school? I shall die for shame.'

'Hey, Miriammon! My father wants to talk to you. It's really important so you'd better hurry. Stop combing your hair.'

Miriammon laid aside the mirror and reluctantly rose to her feet. Pepi wandered back moodily to see how the ants were getting on. Dad was right. He'd be better off with Dad dead than disgraced. For one thing they'd all be sorry for him at school instead of scornful. For another, there'd be a smashing party to look forward to in seventy days' time, like they had for grandma.

Nebankh sat down at his desk like an old man. He slid back the lid of the writing case and selected an unused calamus. Deftly slicing the end at an angle, he nibbled the tip delicately. Before he moistened the ink block he dipped the calamus into water and flicked out a few drops onto the floor as a libation to Imhotep, greatest of scribes. Then he set to work on the most important letter of his life.

Presently Miriammon, his favourite dancing girl, came and stood before him. He turned and gazed longingly at her, transfixed by the delicate beauty of her downcast eyes, but proudly elevated nose. Giving her the letter, he told her to make haste and take it in person to the house of Ptahmose.

Her eyes widened. 'Pharaoh's Ringbearer—the Djaty of the North?'

'The very same.'

He let his tears trickle down his cheek as she left the house, for he knew he would not see her again. In the letter to the Djaty he had stated the facts of the matter, explained that he could not see how to evade disgrace. He begged that the dancing girl be permitted

to find sanctuary in Ptahmose's house and pleaded
with the Djaty to seek ways to punish the wickedness
of Sobekiry.

As the supreme Judge and Inspector General of
the Northern Kingdom, reporting only to the King
Himself, the Djaty could not be seen to be taking
bribes. However Nebankh knew that he would be
pleased with the gift of the girl. It was not as if he were
asking for justice to be perverted. Indeed he was not
asking for justice at all, for Pharaoh's favour is not a
matter of justice. It's a state of grace.

Then he bade farewell to his wife. 'If they send for
me,' he said, 'tell them that I am paying a visit to my
tomb to see how the work is progressing. Say that I
will come tomorrow.'

'If Pharaoh sends for you, surely you'll have to go
straight away?'

'Not if they can't find me.'

He took her two hands in his. 'Whatever happens,
my love, remember this. I would rather die than be
disgraced. So do not think that today you stare
destitution in the face. Console yourself with the
knowledge that you face, at worst, an honourable
widowhood.'

With that he climbed into his sedan chair and the
chair-men bore him off, singing their tired old song:

Better for us
For it to be full
Than empty...

'Tabubu, my girl,' she said to herself, 'it's your misfortune to be married to a failure. He's a loving husband maybe, but a dead loss as an official of the Royal Household. Is there time for me to go to the magistrate and get a divorce for the sake of the children? Otherwise, when Pharaoh sends to undo him, he'll drag us all down with him.'

She went into her boudoir and took up her bronze mirror with its ivory horns of Hathor inlaid with gold. How she wished she had been a little less stick-in-the-mud. Many another wife had a score of admirers to choose from if her husband let her down. Nudging fifty, her looks were still not too bad. Lay the kohl on a bit thicker, widen the eyes back across her temples, a bit more eyeshadow and she'd still be capable of turning a head or two. Perhaps she ought to hurry down to the market to see what she could manage in the time remaining to her.

She was still contemplating her features in the mirror when the anxious maid announced visitors. In the parlour stood two courtiers in white, each holding a jackal-headed cane.

'I'm afraid you've only just missed him...'

'So it seems, my lady.' The courtier beckoned a burly attendant from the doorway and tapped the jug of beer with his stick.

'Tell him we shall call for him at dawn tomorrow. Meanwhile we'll just take this with us, I think.'

*　*　*

Nebankh took the ferry to the western bank and
strode along the path to the terraces cut in the cliff
face. He normally spent a few moment outside his
father's tomb—just long enough to check the seals and
to pour some water on the ground from the small
spouted pot he carried for the purpose—but today he
went straight to the entrance of his own tomb.

Anpur was there as he had hoped, blocking in the
bold figures outlined in red upon the rendered walls.
He glanced over his shoulder and turned his head
smartly away as if the sight of Nebankh pained him.

'Well, my good Anpur, how goes it?'

'Fine, fine.' The graphics designer did not bother
to look round again.

'How near completion is it?'

'What's the panic? You're a young man.'

Nebankh was hard put to explain his anxiety.
Whatever he said, he'd better not tell the truth.

'To tell the truth, I've had a bit of a scare recently.
Good friend of mine, you know. Younger than I
am…'

'What are you trying to tell me, Nebankh? That
you're not happy with my progress?'

'N-no… I—er—I think you're doing a marvellous
job. Keep at it.'

'That's what I am doing. There's been quite a bit
of work undoing the shambles the previous contractor
left this tomb in. Rotten sand trotter, that he was. You
didn't employ me just to get a bit of paint slapped on
the walls, I imagine?'

'No, my good Anpur, of course not...'

'Then, my good Nebankh, have a bit of patience. If you were to die today there's nothing in this tomb that could not be completed well within the prescribed seventy days.'

As far as Anpur was concerned, that concluded the inspection. But Nebankh still hung on, wrestling with something he couldn't express.

'If I were to die tomorrow, I—I'd be distinctly worried, I'm sorry to say.'

Anpur looked round balefully.

'I mean—Tabubu's a perfect dear, but I wouldn't trust her to arrange a burial without being perfectly clear in my own mind how it all goes together. You should have seen the mess she made of her own mother's funeral...'

'I did see the mess you both made of her mother's funeral. It won't happen on this occasion—not if I'm in charge. I've written the whole thing out on a piece of pot which I shall leave in the House of Beauty for reference when the time comes. So... have a nice day, Scribe Nebankh.'

'And you,' muttered Nebankh and turned to go. Everything was in order. He had nothing to complain about and no reason to pester Anpur and prevent him from getting on with his work. What he really craved was reassurance. Whatever the reality, he needed to hear soft words, to be smoothed down like a nervous cat. He wished people would show a little sympathy for a fellow's feelings.

Anpur turned surreptitiously to watch him go until he was out of sight. So that was what was biting him. Impending disgrace. 'If I were to die tomorrow…' He'd heard it all before. Invariably it meant stop work and forget about payment. 'Death lies before me today…' And how does the poem start?

Oh, how my name stinks!

He stirred up a great blob of red ochre on his palette and loaded it onto his reed brush. Taking careful aim at the image of Nebankh saluting hawkfaced Ra-Horakhty, he dashed the blob straight into his patron's eye.

As Nebankh stode out of the tomb he stopped dead in his tracks. A pang of dismay shot through him. There in front of him were two courtiers, leaning on their staffs of office. Behind them stood four burly myrmidons in the dreaded uniform of the Temple of Maat.

'Scribe Nebankh, please come with us. The Djaty requires your attendance without further delay.'

*   *   *

Trembling violently, Nebankh was brought into the presence of the Djaty of the North. He stood before the Judgement Seat, flanked by the two courtiers. Fifty priests of Maat, the enforcers of justice throughout the Two Lands of Kemet, stood to attention on either side. In their hands they held staves for the immediate

51

execution of the Djaty's sentence. Sobekiry stood there also, his face beaming with eagerness.

Nebankh and the Djaty had been at school together, although he had not seen Ptahmose for years, except from a distance at official functions. He was much more portly than he remembered him, looking exceedingly imposing in his starched white apron of office and his priestly shaven head, oiled against sunburn (although he never went anywhere unless carried beneath a canopy).

'Ah, Nebankh. At last we've found you. I was just about to adjourn the court until tomorrow. But perhaps we can get this little business over and done with, eh?'

Instinctively Nebankh grasped his right shoulder with his left hand, in a gesture of distress.

'Yes, your Excellency. I—hope so.'

'I've been charged by his Majesty the King (Life, Wealth and Health be unto Him!) to investigate this little matter of the accounts. Scribe Sobekiry, whom you know, has taken it upon himself to question your competence and—I hesitate to say it—your *integrity*, in dealing with the balance of the household rations, namely two jugs of beer.'

Nebankh began to feel his knees turning to jelly and his heart pounding in a hollow chest. Sweat dripped down his back. Whyever hadn't he hanged himself in the tomb whilst he had the opportunity?

'A small matter you might think,' went on the Djaty, 'but one which has taken up a lot of my time today. Bring on the evidence.'

A porter came forward and placed the jug of beer at the feet of the Djaty.

'Now, Nebankh, would you care to identify this vessel as the one which my officers seized from your house this morning?'

'Yes—yes, your Excellency. That is the one.' Nebankh's mouth was so dry he could barely speak in a whisper.

'Why did you take it home?'

'For—safekeeping, your Excellency. I feared... I feared...'

'That if you left it behind, it might disappear? Very commendable of you. There are a lot of shady characters around nowadays, regrettably even in the Royal Household.'

The Djaty took up a scroll. 'You needn't have bothered, as it happens. I've been studying the copy of yesterday's accounts which Sobekiry has yielded up to me and which I've had occasion to correct. Would you care to cast your eye over the figures and say whether you'd agree with them now?'

The scroll was brought to Nebankh and held before his face. The hieratic script swam about before his eyes, ones and tens tumbling over each other. The letters stood out: 'Life, Wealth, Health!'. Everything else seemed to fade from view. Then the bottom line came into focus. Balance: *two* jugs of beer.

'I have to say,' nodded the Djaty, 'that I cannot see anything wrong with these figures. The two jugs of beer are now accounted for—one was checked into the store yesterday and the other is here. The complaint against you is dismissed.'

Greyness rose like a flooding Nile before his eyes, overwhelming the Djaty, the Court and the face of Sobekiry, wide with amazement. A moment later Nebankh found himself supported under the armpits by the two courtiers, who were lowering him gently onto a stool. Vaguely he heard the voice of the Djaty pronouncing sentence—a hundred lashes and five gashes—for diminishing the *ka* of a respected official of the Royal Household. Just as vaguely he heard the voice of Sobekiry crying out for mercy as two score and ten staves held in the hands of the god-servants of Maat cracked down upon his back. The Djaty had descended from the Judgement Seat and was actually helping Nebankh to his feet.

Putting his arm round his shoulders, Ptahmose accompanied Nebankh out of the double door and into the open air. He was saying 'Nobody ever got stretched out for a simple clerical error. You should have known that. Particularly as the error was in Pharaoh's favour.'

'Yes… yes, your Excellency. Thank you…'

'Don't thank me. I'm only pursuing my calling under the rule of our Lord. Oh, by the way, Miriammon sends her love and says she'd be delighted

to stay. I must say I do admire your taste in dancing
girls.'

With that he gave Nebankh a hefty slap on the
shoulders. Guffawing fit to burst, he mounted his
sedan chair and was borne away. The jug of beer was
carried out in his train.

*   *   *

Back home the wife of Nebankh met him at the porch.
She hadn't gone down to the marketplace after all. She
was wearing her grey widow's weeds. Her face was
devoid of makeup and her hair, normally braided,
beaded and henna-ed to perfection, was dusty and
dishevelled. In place of green eye-shadow there was
grime. In place of kohl there were tears. She hadn't
looked so awful since her mother had died.

Tenderly Nebankh kissed her forehead and she
sobbed against his breast.

'It's all right, Bubi,' he whispered. 'It's All Right!'

Together they slowly unrolled the scroll of
accounts. Suddenly Nebankh's eyes started forth from
their sockets and his jaw sagged open.

'What's this? The old fool Ptahmose has gone and
got it wrong!'

His wits had returned by now. In the peace and
security of his own front porch he skilfully totted up
the figures again and again. Each time he got the same
answer. The balance of the beer column should quite
definitely have been one jug, not two. But someone

55

had added a second stroke in the bottom line beside the first, turning the figure one into two.

'The old fraud!' he exploded. 'I suppose you think you can get away with that sort of thing if you're the Djaty.'

Turning to his wife he added ruefully, 'And I suppose he thinks that a first-class dancing girl is a perfectly reasonable consultancy fee for solving my little difficulty at a single stroke!'

Tears started in his eyes, for the second time that day. 'Not to mention the spare jug of beer!'

A HAND IN THE DARK

I hadn't liked the look of the man from the start. Piggy sort, ate too much dinner. But people who know your name get a sort of power over you. They reckon they can stride up behind you when you're out for a walk, put their hand on your shoulder and all that.

Well, I just ran. He ran too. Beyond a fallen tree the path had slipped away into the burn and there I lost my footing and went crashing into the brambles. I heard his heavy feet coming up fast. But at the very moment he would have been on top of me I realised he had stopped dead.

A sparse presence laid a hand on my head, urging it down. I looked up to see her stretch a bow, then her hand dropped gracefully against her cheek as she let go. I read an Agatha Christie where one Ancient Egyptian shot another—*twang!* Agatha Christie had obviously never seen a man killed with a bow and arrow because it doesn't go *twang*, it goes *swish-snap*, like somebody being caned. They don't die like they do on the telly either. They flap about frantically on their backs, then they give a sort of slithering sob and go out like a fallen ember.

She dropped her bow and a moment later I heard her dragging the body off the path. 'Help me!' she hissed. I got up and lifted the man's feet. A few metres up the slope the bracken gave way and swallowed the man whole, snatching the boots out of my hand. I crouched staring after him. Over the blood surging inside my ears like the water in the gorge behind me, I heard a muffled splash.

I looked up at my protectress. She was a brown slip of a thing, narrow faced like an African woodcarving, dressed in a rough light brown tee-shirt which came halfway down her bare legs.

'What have we done?' I gasped.

'He was a very bad man. I've been watching him for weeks. People think nobody sees what goes on down here.'

Putting her long fingertips on my shoulder she stepped past me to go and pick up her bow. Then, raising her hand to me, she stepped sideways and disappeared.

I panicked and ran all the way back to the caravan. Me mam was there, doing baked beans on the Gaz. She looked at me funny-like but she didn't ask what was wrong. She knew I'd not tell her.

'Don't go off with any strange men,' she said later, out of the blue.

'No, Mam.'

She was a fine one to talk.

∗　　∗　　∗

The next day was bright and sunny and I went back along the Glen. It was as if nothing had happened. I was planning to follow the burn all the way to Frosterley. They told me it went underground at one place. But in a big open space strewn with rocks I felt drowsy and clambered over the rough ground until I was hidden from the path.

Scores of rabbits came out from behind the rocks and hopped around lazily. I wished I had a gun. I lined up my thumbs and said 'blam!' Somewhere near at hand a bird kept up a constant stream of twittering. I put my head back against a rock and shut my eyes, letting the sun seep through my eyelids. A dandelion head bounced off my cheek and I sat up suddenly.

There she was, sitting just above me, swinging her bare feet and smiling. As soon as I smiled back she slithered down to sit beside me, showing her skinny thighs. Then she pulled her tee-shirt over her knees.

'Got over your fright?'

'Yes. But won't they be out looking for him?'

'He doesn't come from around here. Nobody will find him. Nobody will even miss him.'

I thought what huge soft brown eyes she had. Dropping my gaze she sighed and lay back, crossing her arms behind her head. I caught a whiff of pine forests on a sultry evening.

'What's your name?' she said.

With a pang of fear I thought, you shouldn't go telling your name to strangers. 'David,' I said. It was a stupid lie. I could almost hear the man calling my name again. 'Gary—come here, Gary!'

She regarded me gravely. But she only replied, 'Then you must call me Emma. How old are you?'

'Eleven.' That was the truth.

She looked the same age as me, but she didn't say,
and we sat in silence. 'Aren't the rabbits tame,' I
exclaimed. 'They're coming up almost to my feet. I've
never known that happen before.'

'That's because I'm here.'

I laughed. 'Do you look after rabbits, too?'

'Not normally. The birds do that. They warn the
rabbits if there's any danger.'

'Really?'

'Yes. There's a blackbird over there, scolding away
at you. She thinks you're going to shoot them.' She let
out an accomplished trill and the bird shut up.

'Are you on holiday?'

'Kind of. We're here for the whole summer, me
and Mam. The caravan's all she's left with.'

The smile went from her face like the sun going in.
'No dad?'

'Oh, I've had lots of dads.' I was far too casual.
'They come and go. There isn't one at the moment,
but me mam keeps trying.'

'Why did you come here today?'

'I was going to follow the stream right down to
Frosterley. I want to see where it goes.'

Gazing up at the clouds she said in a dreamy voice,
'There's nineteen paths along Rocky Glen. But only
three of them are open to the sky...'

I got up on one elbow and goggled at her.

'Do you scare easily?' she asked.

'No,' I lied. I knew I wouldn't if she was with me.

That afternoon I saw a dark world I had never imagined was there. Some of the tunnels were man made, a deserted city beneath the fell. Others were carved by the stream itself, just the right size for a boy and a girl. Emma flitted through the caves like a living tree root. She couldn't hide her delight in having someone to show them to. And as for me, who'd never held more than an electric torch in the dark, to have a flaming brand to hold was a thrill in itself.

But somewhere in that tangle of caverns a body lay. I kept thinking it would rise up and come after us and lay a sodden hand on my shoulder. Once I tripped and the torch fell in some wet and went out. It was only Emma's fingers holding mine in the utter blackness that stopped my heart bursting out of my chest in shrieking terror.

I lost all sense of direction, but when I emerged blinking through a screen of matted ivy, I found myself in a place I had never seen before. Cliffs scowled down at me on either side.

'Where are we?'

'Harehope Quarry. A hundred men and boys lived by this burn once and mined it for lead and spar. This whole valley is man-made, except for the burn winding down the middle between the weeping willows. It comes back out of the ground over there. Nobody knows where it's been. But I know.'

*   *   *

Next morning I bolted my breakfast and hurried back to the Glen with hardly a word to Mam. I waited for ages among the Rabbit Rocks but Emma didn't come. At last I walked with heavy steps over the footbridge, meaning to stroll back towards the caravans. Over the bridge, in a lovely natural garden, gorse sprouting among the stones, I stood before what looked for all the world like a secret gate in the rock. A naked white tree cast its shadow over the gate and me. My thoughts felt their way along unexplored paths just below the surface of my mind.

Wiry fingers crept into my hand. I turned round to gasp into Emma's sunny face. 'Where've you been?' I accused.

'I've been watching you for hours.'

'That's cruel. I've waited for you all morning. Why didn't you call out to me?'

'You don't have to rush back, do you?'

'Me mam's not expecting me.' I couldn't stop looking at her mahogany eyes.

'That's good,' she said. Without warning she slipped her tee-shirt over her head. As I guessed, it was all she was wearing. She was like an ash sapling in bud. Throwing the tee-shirt in my face she scrambled down to the water's edge and plunged in.

Bollihope Burn goes over a limestone pavement at that point, before tumbling into a wide, placid pool, perfect for swimming in. I didn't dare follow her through the rapids, but I saw she was making for the

pool and there I joined her, slipping out of my clothes
at the water's edge.

'Someone will come!' I hissed.

'There's nobody for miles,' she replied with
absolute conviction.

We splashed and swam for hours. Her brown
limbs gleamed in the dappled sunlight and scorched
marks in my mind. I had been too young to start
thinking about a girl's body, but from then on I'd shut
my eyes at night and picture nothing else.

*   *   *

There wasn't a day throughout July and August I didn't
see Emma. Sometimes me mam wanted us to go out
somewhere and meet Someone Nice, but I pretended
to be sick and stayed in my berth with the curtain
drawn until she was gone. Then I hurried off down the
Glen.

Far too soon it was all over. That afternoon I
knew we'd have to go back to Byker the next day, me
to start school on Monday, Mam to find somewhere
permanent. I thought of asking Emma to run away
with me.

'Have you ever been to Newcastle?'

She gave me a look as if I'd said 'Have you ever
been to Baghdad?' We were shooting toadstools on a
rotten log with her bow. She told me she never shot
anything possessing feelings. Except that one time… I

tingled to the touch of the bow, thinking how it had killed a man.

Dusk fell and I couldn't bring myself to say goodbye. As I faltered she took my arm. 'Have you any biscuits in your caravan?'

Stripped of the woodland's cloak, Emma just looked a scrawny kid with a bow over her shoulder. Mam would say 'Where've you dug her up from?' Fortunately she wasn't in, but as usual she'd locked the caravan. I was good at getting my bedroom window open with a wiggle. Emma was as light as an armful of dry bracken as I slipped her inside to unlock the door.

I opened up the biscuit tin for Emma. She dug down for the last Jammie Dodger, then she sat on the edge of the built-in seat nibbling it and carefully catching all the crumbs. Voices outside. I jumped to the sink window and peered over the sill. It was the people in the caravan opposite, but they didn't look my way. Turning back to Emma—she'd gone. She must have fled through my bedroom window.

It was only when I crept desolate into bed that night that I discovered any sign she'd been. Hidden in the bed were her bow with three arrows and a little pouch with long drawstrings twisted out of grass. Her name was on the bow, scorched in curly pokerwork, and of course it wasn't Emma. Actually I couldn't say really what it was, but it looked like Dyann or Vyviann if you glanced at it quickly.

I tried to keep it hidden but me Mam soon found it and broke it up. 'You could hurt someone!'

If she only knew.

I wore the pouch next to my skin and I never got any colds all winter, but the following spring it fell to bits. I put it on the fire and it flared up mauve and was gone. I thought I saw her face.

Now, five summers later, me mam's got a new caravan, at Stanhope this time. Dad's been with us a couple of years now. We get on champion. Most days Mam and Dad go off together, which suits me fine. One sunny afternoon I took the bus to Frosterley and walked up Rocky Glen. It was quiet and empty. I knew she wasn't there.

DON'T REALLY EXIST

The black-clad policemen went a fraction out of his way and dropped his heel onto a boiled sweet. It was a satin cushion, glinting in the hard light of the mercury lamps, and he turned and looked back at the white fuzz of sherbet. There's one that would never see the inside of some little brat's gob. The pleasure that had given him almost justified the extra few paces added to the straight plod along the promenade. Of course, one couldn't expect real kicks out of a spell of bloody night duty.

Pacing along the cold, deserted promenade—ah, that's the Life For Me. Nothing but the ornamental flagstones; the steel bright street lamps, their mauve, indefinable aura that condensed in ghostly exhalation upon bits of paper; and the dog-fouled railings. Behind the railings—blackness. True blackness. The sea was out there, but one wouldn't have known it. The land stood motionless but for the bustle of the blinking beacons at the crossings, flashing away for a thousand yards to where the traffic lights dozed in *laissez-faire* viridian.

The policeman death-marched towards the covered shelter with its slatted public seating. Little oases these were on the daytime promenade, where old ladies could collapse in contemplation of the sea and let their little pekes run tethered to ensnare a passer-by.

Black arm slid across black chest and the policeman's elbow thumped into a bundle of rags.

'Oof!' said the bundle of rags.

'Psst! Wanna buy a battleship?'

'No thank you, officer,' the bundle of rags replied evenly.

When the policeman had gone it thought to itself, 'Another half-hour's sleep and then I'll really be moved along.'

*   *   *

Daylight, and busy people rose up from the ground like the dew. With all those verticals in translation his static bulk was out of place, but of course he couldn't see it that way. He only felt that he ought to move. Stand up after three hours' sleep, looking as though you have only just sat down—no stretching allowed. It's an art that has to be perfected by practice.

A brief look behind him to see that nothing had dropped off him, then he shuffled slowly away on broken blisters. A man has every right to walk along the promenade—a right guaranteed since the days of King Alfred—but no right to stand still on it. Herbert was conversant with these important points of law and like an obedient citizen he complied, as far as he was able to.

How he wished he had half-a-crown. Herbert stood beside the chrome-plated case and the cigarettes peeked at him tantalisingly through the grid-backed

68

glass front. How he wished that he had been blessed
with half-a-crown—that magic token of metal which
doubtless jingled past him twice a second in smartly
styled trouser pockets, glowing with groin-kindled
heat. He couldn't walk into the shop. He'd be ejected
after the manner of the bits of dog turd that people
bring in on their insteps.

A florin, a few blackened pennies and halfpennies,
and even a farthing. But no half-crown. At least the
farthing would still be there when the rest had gone.
He would keep that—it might be worth quite a bit in a
few years' time.

'Begging your pardon, madam—have you got
changed for two shillings and sixpence?'

Madam didn't even see him. Perhaps she genuinely
hadn't heard what he'd said. 'I must have asked her the
wrong thing', he thought. But she hadn't looked
offended.

As a matter of fact she hadn't looked anything in
particular—just a bit startled.

People flowed along in interpenetrating streams.
Occasionally little eddies separated from the swirling
coiffures and flickering calves and paused to gyrate
before a shop window. Always they looked down at
the window, never up. Herbert wondered why the
shopkeepers bothered to put anything up there at all,
unless it was to hide the sight of all those people
trotting past.

In a recessed shopfront a sleek lad with a foam-
backed iridescent coat wrapped round him like a sheet

of copper turned away from the colourful book covers, the lurid flashes and female backs.

'Excuse me, you young fellow.' That startled look in a face that otherwise failed to admit his presence. But Herbert had him cornered.

'Have you got change for two and six?'

The boy forced himself to look at the sack of garbage barring his way and his face registered surprise that it should conceivably need change for two and six. Herbert felt he had to explain.

'I want a packet of cigs out of the machine and I haven't got half a crown. Haven't had a smoke all week—terrible it is.'

The boy fished awkwardly in his pocket. He poked the required coin into Herbert's stubby hand, against which his own looked smooth and girlish.

'Thanks. Here's the two and six—no, take it!' But the lad was already submerged in the seething sidewalk.

Herbert didn't like it when that happened. He felt he'd just committed armed robbery. Why hadn't the boy taken his money? He could have wrapped it in a bit of paper and washed it when he got home, if he was that worried where it had been. It was just a way of emphasising that the boy had lots of money and that he himself had only two and eightpence three-farthings to his name. He couldn't help being poor. Why did the boy have to accentuate the difference?

The coin was gobbled up by the machine. It said 'Clinkle rattle klong.'

And the cup at the bottom answered 'Clatter.'

Hell to this lousy machine. What was wrong with his flaming money then? He inserted it at the top again, but this time there was no 'clatter'. His guts always froze whenever he lodged all of half-a-crown in one of these inhuman machines. There was no guarantee the machine wouldn't just swallow your money and flatly refuse to give you anything in return. As his hand hesitated on the drawer he thought 'Easy come, easy go. In a few moments you will hammer that machine and then walk away wondering whether you really did put half-a-crown in it—if you hadn't just imagined somebody gave you it. Because everything will be the same as it was a minute ago—you'll be no richer, no poorer… Come to think of it, *did* you put half-a-crown in that machine? No—don't pull the drawer! Until you do, there's the chance the machine really does contain your half-crown. You can't afford to throw away good chances by making them bad certainties.'

An involuntary jerk and the drawer opened. There lay a packet of cigarettes. Herbert was tempted to say 'thank you'—but you don't thank a machine. One of those rules of etiquette.

*   *   *

A deft wrench of the hand without even looking and the crown top dropped among its predecessors with a metallic splash. The landlord slid the black foam into a clear, glittering glass.

'Have you heard this one, Alfie?...' The rest of the little gang of customers drew closer. As the newcomer pushed the bar door and strode in, he was hailed amid howls and chuckles. 'What's all this then?'

'You tell him,' said the policeman, whose off-duty hours were invariably spent propping up the bar.

'This is Micky's joke.' The publican indicated the policeman in mufti. 'What's black on the outside, red on the inside, and you laugh like a drain every time you see it?'

The other customers stopped sniggering and stood waiting in cheerful anticipation of hearing it once more.

'What? Say it again...'

'What's black on the outside...' As the publican repeated the joke syllable for syllable the smiles of the others grew impatient. The newcomer unbuckled his raincoat.

'Good Lord, don't ask me! What is it then?'

'A coachload of niggers going over a cliff.' Vigorous laughter. Previously a nervous overtone had just been perceptible, which was missing this time.

The door of the bar was slowly pushed open and Herbert peered round. It was a funny experience for him. It was as if he were in a film that had stopped dead at one frame. There was something unreal about moving up to the bar when everyone else was standing stationary. It required an intense psychic effort to force himself to keep on walking... nearer and nearer to the bar... where the publican was staring at him...

'Do you think you… I—I mean you could apply—oblige me with a beer?' Herbert's chest was stifled and his tongue suddenly inflamed. 'A half of beer?'

The customers turned away from looking at him and fingered their glasses.

The publican didn't answer for some time. He kept a still face and an eye fixed upon Herbert, which concealed the fact that a series of phrases were passing with juddering rapidity across the nerves leading to his tongue.

…I'm sorry, I don't want your custom… I'm very sorry… we don't serve tramps… we'd be obliged… actually our rules state… there is no facility for… we like a collar and tie… we only have pint mugs—Good God, ease him off somehow!

'Sorry old chap.' The landlord eventually spoke in a conciliatory manner. 'I don't really want you in here.'

When it came to the point, the landlord was blunt and honest. Now the ragbag and the publican stared at each other. Was he going to cause trouble? There'd be no difficulty ejecting him if he did.

Herbert spoke at length. 'Yer…' He turned round mumbling, '…good day' and embarked on the painfully long journey to the door, three yards away.

The publican said thoughtfully to his silent customers, 'I couldn't really serve him. He'd lower the whole tone… he'd… one's got to think of the other customers.'

The policeman poured his beer down his throat and casually applied the face-saver. 'Oh, we know all about that fellow. He turns up in the district every now and again, just arsing around.'

The others looked at him to continue.

'Sleeps rough. He's got a record for malingering. We know him well at the station.'

One of the customers was being mesmerised by the temptation to run outside and cry 'Come back!' He could take him into the other bar and stand him a pint. But after Micky had finished speaking he was relieved to feel the irrational notion evaporate.

Much later, when he had locked the doors, the landlord had to tell his wife the whole story. Then he too was able to forget it.

*   *   *

Herbert plodded his way along the promenade, his practised eye open for discarded dog-ends or a sweet lying about on the flagstones. There was one squashed back there. Why did people have to squash them?

Bit of a nerve that was—going into a pub to celebrate his new-found wealth. He knew they wouldn't serve him. So he bought a pie instead at a little boutique, badly straining the conscience of the young miss behind the hatch. The Hygiene Act was her ethical code (quite right too!) and a loathness to touch his money all but prevented her, too, from serving him.

Herbert sat down on a bench looking out over the sea and devoured his pie. The ball of meat fell out and he had to grovel under the bench for it, among bits of paper, grit and dried stains. Herbert was a connoisseur. He knew that this didn't improve the flavour at all.

Having dined, he sat back and watched the hurrying crowd. What were they all hurrying for anyway, and he sitting still? It was as if the fact of sitting still in a moving world somehow denied one any existence in that world. He could stand in the middle of a flow of people and nobody would notice him. Except that they never seemed to bump into him. Perhaps he just couldn't observe that they were actually walking through him. Most of the time it seemed as if they were giving him a big space all of his own. He was in an entire dimension all his own.

'All these people!' he declaimed loudly. One person actually glanced at him. Marvellous! Perhaps he really did exist. Or maybe it was the other way round. In reality he himself existed, the rest were all part of his imagination.

'All these people—trudging to the mines with their shovels on their backs.' A prim lady with a crocodile handbag treated him to a sour glance.

'Yes, she was a pretty young girl once,' announced Herbert, entirely for his own benefit.

New blue anorak and thin black trousers. A lad of about twenty went by, striding with a sea-invigorated air.

'Hey you, young fellow. Come over here.' Herbert wanted to ask him what all the hurrying was about. He got a direct glance for a moment, but the lad was glancing about at random and it was probably just a coincidence that their eyes met. But he did seem to glance away with a jerk.

A quarter-of-an-hour later a black Wolseley, carrying a loudspeaker in front of the radiator, pulled up at the kerb. Two policemen got out.

'Wonder who they're after,' thought Herbert idly. They moved as if wading through treacle, preoccupied with some private grief. A moment later, with a start, Herbert found them standing either side of him.

'Causing a nuisance again, Herbert. People have been complaining about you.' The voice was flat and routine and so was the ride to the cells. The supper he got was a lot worse than usual.

In the morning they took him outside and sat him in the black Wolseley again. Up the long wide St. Helen's Road, with a lovely view of Scots pines in the sunken park, out into Sedlescombe Road North, up towards the Ridge… he knew it all.

The car stopped. The constable reached across him and opened the door onto ditch and bushy hedgerow.

'Get out and keep walking. We don't want to see you in this town again.'

They sat and watched Herbert stumping slowly westwards towards Eastbourne.

THE KATZENDOPPELGÄNGER

My cat believes in ghosts.

I can guess what you're thinking—how can I possibly know that? I know because she has actually seen one. No, I must confess I never saw it myself. But other people have. And the cat of course—she saw it loads of times, from the very first day she came to us.

My children had been pestering me for a cat, so when I could stand it no longer I put an advert in the post office window:

Kitten Wanted by Good Home and Loving Family.

'Oh, if only I'd known,' said the post-lady. 'Our neighbour went and drowned his two kittens last Saturday.'

I emerged from the shop fuming, but maybe it was a blessing in disguise. How would I have responded to 'Have whichever you like—I'm going to drown the other one'? I'd have ended up with two kittens instead of one.

We didn't have to wait long for a reply to our advert. But what arrived wasn't a kitten at all. A distraught lady came and went again in tears, having left us a cat. A full-grown cat, plus tins of cat food, cat litter, tray, basket, carrying cage—in fact a complete ready-to-stroke cat kit for beginners.

'She's called Cinders. You won't believe me, but she's five years old.'

I stared in amazement at the shrunken animal as it cowered in a corner. Tortoiseshell she was supposed to be, but she had the colour and texture of a bad banana.

'I think we chose the wrong one. The weaker of the two.'

I recalled out loud what the postmistress had told me. 'Yes,' said my visitor. 'I was put in that spot, too. I just said "eeny meeny miny mo" because I couldn't see any difference. I wish I'd looked a little closer, now. But she's got such a sweet nature. Perhaps I made the right choice after all...'

She stopped and thought about that.

'There again, perhaps you'd say I shouldn't have had either kitten. But then they'd both have been drowned.'

Well, what could I do? I accepted the pathetic creature. The lady would accept no payment. She knelt and kissed the cat's head and tears fell on its fur. Then she got up and went out of our lives.

When you acquire a second-hand cat you expect some compensation for it being no longer a kitten. So I was glad to discover that she was house-trained. We cut a cat flap in the back door, but would she go out on her own? She would not. Not unless I stayed near-at-hand. On guard, as I suspected. Whenever I went outside she would follow me around everywhere I went. It gradually began to dawn on me that the cat was obsessed.

I mean possessed. Haunted.

During the day her accustomed place was on the window ledge. There she would keep watch on the outside world. She never sat, but would crouch, tail twitching, ready to spring. Then all of a sudden she would leap down and tear round the room like a demon, clinging to the furniture with her claws, bounding off like an arrow from a bow and ending up cowering beneath the sideboard.

She never let the children touch her, which made her a great disappointment. And she rarely slept. A normal cat, a vet once told me, snoozes for near on twenty hours a day, more like a piece of upholstery than a living companion, but that would have been fine by me. If I had wanted a restless, fidgety pet, I told myself, I'd have done better to advertise for a goldfish. Or a budgerigar. You just let it peck its mirror all the time.

That gave me an idea. Perhaps she was lonely and would welcome the sight of a friendly furry face. I always did, every morning, when I went for a shave. One day I fetched the bathroom mirror and gave her a glimpse of herself.

I might have tossed a bomb. Cinders let out a shriek—until then I had not heard her so much as mew. Ears flat, she snarled and folded up like a concertina. Then she bolted for the window, shot straight up the curtain and cowered on top of the pelmet, hissing. There was no getting her down. We had to leave her there till next morning.

*　　*　　*

I was outside, weeding my patch of front garden. Joe from down the road walked past, his poodle padding along in front.

'You'll get wrong off Mrs Hobart,' he tossed at me.

'What have I done now?'

'It's your new cat. Been scratching in her lettuces. Not to mention jumping on the bird table and eating the bacon rinds put out for the blue tits.'

'Never!'

'There's no mistaking your cat, with those hind legs, one black and one white.'

I went back indoors and called my children. 'Have you ever known Cinders go out?' I asked. 'No,' they assured me. Nevertheless to give her a cast-iron alibi we all kept careful watch on Cinders for the next few days.

*　　*　　*

Look at that!' said Mrs Evans.

'Poor Snowy,' I crooned. 'Who did that to you?'

'That was your cat as did that,' she said, plucking Snowy's split ear from my fingers.

'I can't believe it! She never goes out if she can possibly help it. You must be mistaken.'

'I saw it with my own eyes. I'd know your cat anywhere. And do you know what else it's done…?'

And so it went on.

I began to get paranoid about the neighbours, but that was nothing to Cinders' state of mind. She used to claw frenziedly at the door jamb if we left her in the lounge when we went to bed. Eventually we relented and let her sleep on our bed. We provided cat litter in the kitchen and she gave up going outside altogether.

Until one day she took off.

She had been crouching in her usual position of vigilance on the window ledge when she spotted something. The back door was open and all of a sudden she leapt down and streaked outside in a single movement. We waited all that day and all the next, but there was no sign of her. I put another advert in the post office window, but this time it said LOST CAT.

Days passed, until one morning as I was getting the tea I heard a scratching at the window frame. I opened up and in plopped Cinders on her front paws, purring her greetings and nuzzling my leg. She ate a whole tinful of catfood in three noisy, greedy minutes and then curled up and went to sleep in front of the fire for the rest of the morning. Such nonchalance! Not that I really expected any explanation.

*   *   *

Joe knocked at the door. 'Just thought I'd look in to tell you. I spotted your cat this morning…'

His eyes widened in amazement to see Cinders flopped out on the mat. 'Well I never! So you've got her back? When did she turn up?'

We compared times. 'She must have come straight back here after I saw her.' He scratched the back of his neck. 'Well…! If there's such a thing as a cat getting done for murder, yours would be up for a long stretch.'

'What on earth do you mean?'

'I saw her and another cat on the parapet of the bridge down the bottom.'

'What were they doing?'

'Fighting…' He looked at me as if I had the nerve to ask.

'How did you know it was mine?' I asked.

'No mistaking it, is there? One hind leg's black and the other's white. Have you ever seen another cat like it?'

I shook my head. But to my surprise Joe craned his neck in a mysterious sort of way. 'Well I have. The other cat was like it. Exactly like it. They might have been twins. Well just as I came up, yours took an almighty swipe at the other and knocked it clean off the parapet. I ran to look but saw no sign of it, not even a ripple. Must have gone straight to the bottom.'

'The poor thing! At least it sounds like it didn't suffer much.'

'No… That's if it was really there, of course.'

'What are you on about?'

'I mean—the whole thing happened so suddenly, I wondered afterwards if I hadn't imagined it. There was no sound. Unusual for cats fighting. It was like—shadow boxing…' His voice tailed off momentarily. 'I must say your cat was right pleased with itself. Licked its paw as if to say "That Made My Day!"'

*   *   *

The children and I sat round staring at Cinders, who blinked back at us dozily.

'So that's what was wrong the whole time,' said Gillian, my eldest. 'There was a nasty, mean cat out there and you were afraid to go outside. Now it's gone. Gone and you're back to normal.'

'What's normal about that cat?' I asked.

'Everything. She eats, snoozes all day, goes for a prowl outside when she fancies. She takes us for granted, 'cept when she wants something to eat. She lets me stroke her now. Look.'

'I can see that,' I agreed. 'You wouldn't think she was the same cat.'

'Don't be silly! Of course she is.' Gillian always took things so literally. 'Look at her back legs. How many other cats could there possibly be with a black left leg and a white right leg?'

'No,' said Lucy. 'You've got it the wrong way round. I know—' she said as Gillian protested, "cos I sat and drew Cinders the other day.'

Lucy fetched her drawing book.

83

'You might have drawn her outline,' snorted Gillian over my shoulder, 'but you must have shaded it in later and got it wrong.'

Must she? I wondered. My eyes went from the cat to the picture, then back to the cat. Picture–cat… Picture–cat. As they hopped to and fro I began to feel the hairs rise beneath my shirt collar. For the picture was indeed the spitting image of the cat which lay purring before us.

The mirror image.

INNER SPACE

*Heaven is separated from the Earth by empty
space, yet it does not fall in. It is like a bellows:
work it—and ten thousand things will issue forth.
Speak into it—and ten thousand words will die
away. It is good to preserve some inner space.
(Tao Te Ching, c. 2300 BCE).*

Fifty milligrams of fulminate of mercury packed into a
hand-cast slug sprayed Lao-Tan's brains around the
lavatory walls. But Lao-Tan was out of his body at the
time, concentrating on locating Carlos and his
myrmidons. However they had discovered him first,
squatting lotus-like, insensible to his surroundings. He
came back to find his wrecked corpse crumpled on the
tiles in a mess of blood.

A moment's inattention is rarely of consequence
to ordinary people. But if you are a *chen-jen*, a Great
Soul, it is invariably disastrous.

How easy it would have been to melt away
forever. But hesitating on the threshold of non-
existence Lao-Tan turned back, choosing to remain
earthbound. The consequences of such an act would
be appalling. But to have conceded victory to Carlos
would have vitiated the achievements of a thousand
lives. He fled across the car park to an unmarked side
door. Without stopping he passed through it as though
it were immaterial.

It was a fire escape door at the bottom of a flight of stairs, up which he now floated. At the top, behind another door, a dimly-lit ward stretched away into shadows. Encumbered sleepers lay in silent ranks, each garlanded with tubes and coloured wires. No motion of breathing disturbed the graveyard calm.

Not a nurse was in sight: forget the idea that an Intensive Care Unit is patrolled unceasingly by Florence Nightingales in soft shoes and dark woollen cloaks. Only the whining of an alarm on a vital instrument makes one appear, later if not sooner.

An instrument was whining now. A disembodied soul, confused and terrified, stood trembling by one of the beds. Straightaway Lao-Tan was at her side. Embracing the soul he kissed her passionately and, whirling round with her, he hurled her heavenwards. Then glancing round to see if he was being watched he slipped inside the cast-off body.

The soul sped upwards in delirious bliss. In a thousand years she would fall back to Earth and be reborn. Lovely, intelligent and resourceful, she would spend her life roaming the Earth and the inner planets looking for Lao-Tan, but she would never find him.

*　　*　　*

'Check the records, Dr Masrur, for any patient resuscitated between nine o'clock last night and six this morning. Inject them with this. If anyone gets suspicious, we'll make it all right for you.'

'Your wish is my command.'

'Oh—and all babies born in the same period too. No hurry with those. Just get them recalled to hospital for a routine examination. I'll give you a fungal preparation that doesn't act for a week or two. It'll look like a cot death.'

The third man shrugged. 'Hey Boss! I saw you blow that funny old chink's head off. Why all the fuss?'

Carlos sighed as if surrounded by one fool too many. 'Some people, Stefan, are not so easily got rid of.'

*　　*　　*

A heart fibrillating like a bowl of worms. Blood draining down to the dorsal region and congealing. A liver digesting itself in its own bile. In life the *yang* of anabolism balances the *yin* of catabolism. But at death *yang* ceases, leaving *yin* to persist and so return the body to the earth.

Lao-Tan exerted his *yang* to the utmost, sending the message that once more someone was in command. Gradually proteins untwisted, muscles began to twitch and nerves to flicker. Presently traces appeared on the screens clustered on a nearby trolley.

Lao-Tan bellowed into the void which separates Heaven from Earth, though no sound emerged from his borrowed lips. But the cosmic jolt started the heart beating once more. Like a flame struck by a spark upon a windy heath, Lao-Tan cupped it and nursed it,

87

pouring into it his astronomical reserves of creative love.

A nurse came in haste. Where had she been when the alarm went off? What could she have done anyway but interfere? Guiltily she felt the patient's pulse, listened to the breathing, consulted the instruments and silenced the alarm. There had been a crisis but it had passed. Maybe it was just a feint, the real death blow to arrive in the next few hours—or minutes? But for the present the patient was in a stable condition and she hurried off again. The incident was not recorded. Which was why it didn't come to the attention of Dr Masrur.

Lao-Tan sighed with his newly acquired lungs and gingerly extended his astral limbs into the resurrected body. He felt the agony of pneumonia, the stabbing pain of restored circulation, the excruciating headache of breakdown products in the blood. In all this he luxuriated, knowing they signified he was alive. To respond as they demanded he writhed and groaned. But in his inner space he laughed.

It was only now that he discovered the crushing disabilities the dead girl had endured in life. Quadriplegia. Down's Syndrome. The intelligence of a two-year-old. On top of it all her heart was degenerate, her liver defective and she only had one functioning kidney.

It takes an ocean of mental energy for the mind to break free of the physical body, to construct an avatar on the astral plane and inhabit it. Energy which this damaged brain would have enormous difficulty in channelling. He was trapped inside this crippled body, every bit a prisoner as its late owner had been.

*   *   *

But Lao-Tan made good progress and they transferred him to his own side room in the Female Medical Ward. There he would grunt to indicate that he needed to perform some bodily function, but without anyone getting the message. The staff found it more convenient to let him lie in his own mess until they got round to mopping him up.

Two days later he had a visitor. A man came and stared down at him. Gazing into those despairing eyes he knew that he was face-to-face with the dead girl's father.

What could he see in those eyes? Loathing? Yes: the man had never overcome the loathing of having fathered a deformed child. Resentment? Yes: resentment at the chains which shackled his life.

What about hatred? No: there was no actual hatred to be seen. Here was a man endowed with little natural virtue, who by force of will had shouldered the burden of a retarded child. Here was the man whom Lao-Tan was fated to be totally dependent upon.

'Wouldn't it have been kinder to let her die?'

The nurse, taking blood pressure, replied 'We aren't authorised to terminate her life you know. We

89

can't just switch her off. She's not on life support now.'

'Yes but why go to all the effort of resuscitating her when she was clearly dying of pneumonia?'

'My sister-in-law was on Intensive Care that night. She said she didn't intervene. Trixie had a crisis—yes, but she pulled through all by herself. We can't take the blame for that, I mean the credit.'

PATIENCE, MY FRIEND. I SHALL BE A BURDEN ON YOU NO LONGER THAN MY MISSION DEMANDS.

*   *   *

Ten days later they let the father take his daughter home.

Trixie—so that's what he was called. The father's name took longer to discover. He tried to read it from the man's eyes, but they were ground matt with extended suffering and no longer reflected who he really was.

The two of them lived by themselves in a fifth-floor flat which the social services had converted with white-enamelled rails, hoists and special chairs, bath and bed. Around these appurtenances Lao-Tan's life now revolved.

They had very few visitors, but one day a woman opened the front door with her own latchkey and called down the corridor 'George…?'

'George' had just nipped out for a packet of cigarettes (his third that day) so the door closed again. The woman didn't come back.

It was not as if George was ever away for long. He had nobody to cover for him. He took his duties seriously: far more seriously than he took his own health. Trixie was his entire life—his career—his whole reason for being. His official occupation when they asked him: paid carer for his own disabled child. He patiently fed his 'daughter' with a spoon.

Lao-Tan was distressed by how badly he was able to retain food in his mouth. He was not sure which muscles to tighten in order to swallow. But evidently Trixie had displayed no greater skill, for George expected no better of him.

George didn't eat much himself. He subsisted on cigarettes and pork pies. Plus beer: great twelve-packs of the stuff. He'd crash into the living room carrying them under his arm, his hands dragged down by plastic shopping bags. He'd dump them on the floor beside the ever-running television, then he'd collapse into his greasy armchair, springs going clonk, extract a can and brandish it at Lao-Tan.

'Here we are. Here's what makes it all bearable. You can't manage the stuff you great lump of crippled flesh so you won't mind if I finish the lot.'

Then he'd smile, inviting a response. Lao-Tan found it hard to come up with the behaviour expected of him, no doubt long worked out between Trixie and her father. He had to keep telling himself to follow

George's facial expressions and his body language, ignoring the content of what he had actually said.

All too well he knew that Trixie's brain did not possess the power of speech. She would have responded to her father's gestures only, with an exaggerated frown—a grimacing grin—a growl—a hoot.

*　　*　　*

One evening George leaned forward to change channels. He'd lost the control box down the side of the chair. 'Never mind the news. Let's have a bit of sport.'

But tonight the news was of utmost importance. Lao-Tan needed to hear it through. For the first time he would have to take charge of George's will. He felt a deep revulsion at doing so. Just like him, George was a man-of-destiny: a hero, in his sad, pathetic way. But once the higher decision is taken, the man-of-destiny sacrifices further power of choice. His perspective becomes that of Heaven.

LEAVE THE SET ALONE. Lao-Tan silently projected the wish with all the power at Trixie's disposal. There was a fund of naked willpower: a baby's full complement in fact. LEAVE THE SET ALONE.

George slumped back into his armchair. 'Oh let's just carry on listening to the news. Too much effort to fiddle with the damn thing.'

Jo Mobulu, the Lavinian president, was about to meet the rebels. Or rather, the most vociferous of the rebellious factions. His delegation would fly out of Luton tomorrow, bound for Geneva, where talks were to take place under the auspices of the United Nations.

Lao-Tan stiffened. This was precisely what Carlos and his paymasters were at pains to prevent. There was only one possible response. Carlos' stock-in-trade: hijack the aircraft and assassinate the delegation—and to do it in such a manner as to point the finger at a minority faction.

But it would trigger an explosion of violence that would stun the world with horror. And that would only be the start of it. For an outright winner to emerge was something one or other of the onlookers would find intolerable. So the nations of the world would queue up to send their young men in columns for sacrifice on yet another flaming altar, making ashes of their budding hopes and ideas for a better future. Cracked skulls grinning in the mud would mock the broken promise of the New Age.

It must not happen. Lao-Tan concentrated his will to a single point of infinite brilliance. IT WILL NOT HAPPEN.

*   *   *

The next day dawned bright and clear. George's shrill alarm clock woke him to another joyless round, which he commenced as usual by bathing his daughter. By

93

making sure she was washed and perfumed he conferred one single pleasing dimension upon her. To Lao-Tan this was the only pleasure of inhabiting Trixie's stunted body and he grimaced with glee, as he knew she would have done.

'Trixie my girl, ha-ha, they're cutting our benefit.' He grinned fiercely at Lao-Tan, contradicting the content of what he was saying. 'I can't go on. They'll take you into a home. I doubt they'll have the time to do all this for you there.'

He hoisted Lao-Tan onto the drying table and dabbed and coddled his daughter's body with thick warm towels. 'I expect you'll be happier. Who knows? The only reason you're not there already is because I'm here to look after you.' He carried on drying the crippled flesh in silence. 'As for me, well… I'll get me life back, won't I?'

He stopped and stood in thought. 'What'll I do with it?' He went on with the drying. 'Haven't the foggiest. Mebbes I'll drop meself off the bridge.' He barked with laughter, just to swamp any hint in his face of the terrible thing he'd just said.

They sat over breakfast, which for Lao-Tan was a mash of bread and milk and Marmite, patiently spooned in as usual. For George it was the first beer of the day. Winter sunlight streamed through the grubby steel-framed window onto George's face. He closed his eyes.

YES GEORGE, LET THE CLEAN SUNLIGHT WASH OVER YOU. LET IT

PURIFY YOU FOR WHAT WE HAVE TO DO.

'Oh we've not had a bright day like this for yonks. But I bet it's cold outside. If it was summer we could spend the day up on the roof, you and I. But I reckon I'll just wheel you once round the block for a spot of fresh air.'

LET'S GO UP ON THE ROOF.

'On second thoughts let's go up on the roof anyway. We might have it to ourselves. I couldn't face meeting anyone today.'

At the 19th floor the lift door, dented, scuffed and scrawled, opened straight onto the flat roof, where residents could hang a bit of washing or laze in a deckchair and forget they were in the middle of a conurbation. But George's wish was not to be granted. There were people there already: two old dears making the best they could of the scarce daylight. One got up from her deckchair to help George lift the wheelchair down the step. He didn't need help—and she wasn't in a fit state to give it anyway—but they feigned cooperation.

In the sky to the north-west a tiny gleam appeared. Presently the vapour trail could be made out of an airliner as it climbed steeply out of Luton. The Lavinian delegation was on board that plane. So was Carlos.

LIFT ME ONTO THE BALUSTRADE.

A sudden gust flung George's hair about. 'Whee! It's clear enough to see for miles. Of course you can't see it. You can't see much down there can you? Let me lift you onto the balustrade. Just this once mind 'cos it's not safe.'

The plane was now overhead.

KISS ME GEORGE.

Without ever knowing why, George did. For an instant his knuckles lost their whiteness. But that instant was all that Lao-Tan needed. Jerking sharply, he span himself round, out of George's grasp.

'Trixie!'

The two old ladies staggered to their feet as George's scream faded away in the void beneath his outstretched arms and the ground.

Lao-Tan had twisted his body to face skywards, his gaze locked on the airliner, as far as Trixie's feeble eyes would permit. At the moment of impact he let himself spurt upwards in a single tiny drop of life. Caught in the updraught between the tower blocks he was presently wrapt heavenwards in a lofty thermal. The image of the aircraft grew and grew until it filled his droplet.

*   *   *

Carlos had booked the entire row of seats on both sides of the gangway so nobody could see what he was doing. He was assembling his machine pistol from all-plastic parts sewn into his clothing. He slid twenty bullets out of the heels of his shoes, inserting them one by one into the magazine. Then he slipped off the safety catch.

Now let the fun begin!

Something made him look up: something small which had spattered on the window. As he gaped it spread out into a transparent form: an ancient slant-eyed face with a wispy beard. The face of the mystery man who had been hunting him down across the world: the man he had killed with an explosive bullet!

In terror he fired at the apparition. Spent cartridges spun away as the feather-light weapon squirmed in his grasp. Instantly the air rushed past his ears, slamming his face into the rent he'd made.

There it stuck fast, but only for a second. Steadily his head was sucked into an oval maw rimmed with shark's teeth of splintered Plexiglass. The space between the window panes filled with globs of clear red liquid and a narrow cone of body fluids sprayed along the fuselage.

Jowls frosting over in the chilling gale, his eyeballs popped and were snatched away. Then bit by bit, his clothes scraping off and his bones crunching to needles, he was voided from the aircraft like a great big gory turd.

He came down on mud flats in the Thames estuary. They never found his body. It wouldn't have been a very nice thing to find.

As the aircraft levelled out after its emergency descent, the passengers took their noses out of dangling oxygen masks and breathed plain air. Their buffeted ears screamed, their crimson eyes smarted and they felt very sorry for themselves. But when the

captain told them what little was known about the man
who had just been squeezed through the burst
window, a little space was made in their hearts for that
ill-fated individual.

*   *   *

As the first of the bullets struck the window, Lao-Tan
had flaked off and floated down ever-so-slowly in the
sunlight and the blue. A translucent babyform, spread-
eagled in an all-encompassing embrace, he tumbled
gleefully head-over-heels.

Ten thousand brilliant clouds billowed up around
him, fleecy rugs laid wall-to-wall as it were, from
horizon to horizon. Sierras of snowy vapour, they
hung between Heaven and Earth: a space, for all their
vastness, they could never fill.

But the tiny head of Lao-Tan had space for just
one thought: what a beautiful world! What a
beautiful… beautiful… world!

Weeks later he fell into deep forest, far from
human habitation. Trickling rains washed him from a
spiny pinnacle probing the turbid mist, down between
pine needles rotting on the ground into crumbly black
earth reeking of truffles and tombs. There he lay still as
moon followed moon. But when it was spring he
pushed out a single threadlike mycelium.

Ten thousand springs were to come and go before
he once more began to evolve.

98

NO SUPPER FOR SODDY

He is on his back behind metal bars like a little animal
at a zoo. His eyes are open, but looking at nothing.
When his eyes close, he shuts up, but otherwise he
wails—little panting sobs too monotonous to be
pitiful. The bedclothes are pulled down to reveal a tiny
oval body with stunted limbs lying on a wet drawsheet.
From neck to crutch the skin is covered in dense
brown freckles, so close in parts as to leave no white
between. Only it is not freckle. The brown skin is dead
and coarse.

'Had that since he was two. Paraffin heater did
that. Doesn't heal up at all. Born normal.'

'How old's he now?'

'Ten. Looks no older than two, doesn't he.
Shouldn't be alive.'

*　*　*

The woman in white coat and red belt rattles the cot
side down. A voice assails her from the doorway.

'Don't spend too long on that child. I know he's a
slow feeder, but we're way behind with the feeding.'

'Yes, Sister.'

The owner of the voice disappears back into the
office and the little moaning mouth is teaspooned full
of mashed egg-and-potato.

Nothing.

No attempt is made to swallow it and the food is spooned out again.

'Give him some egg-and-milk, then. Get something down him, poor little mite.'

'Used to be on drip feed where he came from, but the doctor said he should come off it.'

'Can't keep them on drip feed indefinitely, you know.' White coat with blue pips on the shoulder picks up a basin to feed the kids outside. The nursing assistant continues to labour in vain, and eggy milk is spluttered over the pillows.

Children are bathed and put into the empty beds around. They sit up and chew the blankets, make grotesque movements with the fingers, or rock and emit uncouth, perfectly rhythmic noises. The few more alert children grin at the staff wheeling the patients in from the bathroom, and point to the blanket trailing on the floor, which it shouldn't do. But the cot in the corner stands neglected until the Big Change, when down come cot sides in turn with a crash... back with the bedclothes... wet sheets and nappies are changed and the red rubber mackintoshes wiped dry.

'You've vomited again!'

The nursing assistant in white jacket and apron and blue-black trousers apostrophically addresses the little patient, whose only response is to cringe up sluggishly and wail. Mental staff always talk to their patients; it's only normal patients in general wards that are treated like cabbages.

'Poor little bugger. He shouldn't be alive. Did he condescend to eat anything today, do you know?'

'Must have done, to bring that back.'

Carefully, but without hesitation, the linen drawsheet is detached from the bed around the slimy pool and wrapped over it. It's not a pleasant job cleaning up catarrhal vomit. At first it's utterly nauseating. But after a while the bad experiences become just spells of distastefulness, which any job has.

'There. Now you've got all night to mess *that* up.'

The grotesque little doll is set in clean linen once more. They give the trolley a nudge and it rolls up the gangway, stopping with a jolt against a bed leg. Filthy water from a basin on the lower shelf slops on the floor and a skinny little face opposite chuckles.

'Blast!'

'Blast'—the word is echoed quietly but distinctly from the end of the ward. One of the men looks round, eyes narrowing. The child in question is paying no attention to anything beyond his extended fingers, jabbing the thumbs against his lips. His eyes roll upwards under the lids and he looks utterly incapable of any response to the outside world at all.

'Get down, Lee.' A snarl from one of the men and surprisingly enough he does—like a flash! Right under the bedclothes, then his head pops out again onto his pillow, not timidly, but as if he hasn't the slightest idea why he dived down so suddenly. Nor does he care. He carries on with his finger exercises as before, stopping

occasionally to declaim total nonsense in a perfectly
enunciated Oxford accent and a pedantic tone of
voice. Types like him, with perfectly good parrot
memories, but little else, are rare. In his case it was
thought to be due to prenatal brain damage when his
mother, a respected academic, contracted German
measles.

'Evening, Mr Relf.'

'Oh, 'allo, Mr Soddy.' The nursing assistant carries
on tucking in the bottom of the bed.

'Got 'em all finished, have you? Jolly good—hang
on a minute and I'll get me apron on, then you can go.
Have the 'off duties' gone up yet?'

'No, Sister hasn't done them all yet. But I've had a
look in the office and you've got two split duties next
week when you come off nights.'

The other man glances aside and says 'F…ff'
through his teeth. Then he is gone in the direction of
the staff lockers. A red-belted woman comes back with
a tray of milk-spattered plastic beakers. Relf says, 'I
suppose we'd better wash these up before we go, Mrs
Wirrall.'

'I tried little David in the corner…'

'Oh, no, you don't need to bother about him.
You'll never get any milk down him in a month of
Sundays.'

'Poor little mite. Has he actually eaten anything
today?'

'Don't know.'

$$*\quad*\quad*$$

'Who do you think's doing the rounds tonight, Arden?' says Soddy, his soft voice deafening after the silence. Miss Arden, in crisp clean white coat and red belt, peeps into the dark, quietly-simmering ward. One cannot see far by the light of the dim beehive bulb, so really she is listening.

What a change these wards are from the geriatric wards, with their restless old folk. Not a sound out of the kids. The reason is that they are all under sedation, doped to the gills with Largactil for the night, but she expects to see one or two of the older boys sitting up in bed sooner or later. She turns to face the kitchen door.

'Tuesday, today, isn't it? Then it will be the night superintendent. Better keep out of the kitchen until she's been round. Then we can have supper.'

'Supper' was an unofficial institution on that ward. It was cooked up from ward rations thoughtfully indented for by Sister, whether they were going to be needed for patients or not. This took place after the late-night bed-change, when there was nothing to do for a while.

'I reckon,' suggests Soddy, 'that someone should be down in the babies' ward when she comes.'

'You go. Last time I trod on a cockroach.' She shudders as she recalls the 'scrunch'.

'There's mice in the kitchen,' volunteers Soddy, but it is no good. '...All right, I'll go.'

He wanders through the playroom, with its familiar sweetish tang of faeces masked with aerosol freshener. It is scarcely perceptible with the windows open, except when you first pass through after coming on duty. The thick green lino, with its congealed tacky layer of who-knows-what, sticks to rubber soles and crackles as you lift your feet. Anyone walking softly in that quiet ward is perfectly audible throughout the whole building. He would have no trouble hearing when the night superintendent came.

*   *   *

The pair of them didn't get their supper that night. They missed their official break, too, standing around uselessly, helplessly most of the time. Hushed bustle in the corner of the ward meant that every young patient who chanced to wake stayed that way. Mouth noises and the occasional voluntary breath implied that half the ward was awake. Every now and again Soddy or Arden left the busy corner to feel their way between beds in answer to a murmur. The night superintendent, a thin woman in dark green, like a cucumber with a paper doily perched on top, insisted on having the screens round, although it was hardly necessary in the dark. The two nursing assistants had to squeeze silently between bed, screen and black gas cylinder in its waist-high trolley, while the night superintendent handled the rubber mask as if she was trying to fit a tyre onto a

Lambretta as it was being inflated. It blew, sneezed and sighed in her grasp.

'Carry on doing this, Mr. Soddy. I'm just going to phone over and hurry up the house doctor.'

*   *   *

The day doesn't dawn. Really it is the night that fades. Night is something tangible; it is black and warm, close and quiet. It settles like a thick fall of dark snow. But then the black snow melts and drains into the corners and its veil is removed from the beds, the ward, the world. Their outlines are now too distinct to be ignored; the blanket is gone and they are naked, cold and colourless. Without night, the world is dead and empty in the first blank realisation of twilight.

Now the business during the night is finished and buried under the activity of the brightening day. Soddy and Miss Arden feel like ghosts that must disappear at cockcrow. Then they realise that they are solid and that the increasing light is not causing them to evaporate in their tiredness, but condensing them, driving them to increasing labour like a match which flares fiercer and brighter before consummation. The ward must be changed, the soiled linen bagged up and placed outside for collecting, the breakfasts prepared and the feeding started; all in the last three hours of night duty. And the little cot with the screen round it stands neglected in the corner.

Enter Relf, fresh out of a nice warm bed.

'…Which is where I shall be in an hour,' thinks Arden as she shovels a mess of bread, milk and porridge into a gaping mouth, spoon clicking on teeth.

The sight of the screen surprises him. He slips behind it. There is little David lying on a single sheet, all nice and clean for once; no spittle or vomit over his cheeks. His mouth and eyes are plugged with cotton wool carefully tied down with white tape. Incongruously a pink rose protrudes from the folded fingers. This is the 'last office', performed to the letter. Relf comes out from behind the screen. He is thinking guiltily, 'No more having to waste time feeding him.'

'Poor little bugger. But I suppose it's about time…'

Arden doesn't answer.

EARTHSPOT

'Whisht! lads, haad your gobs, an' aa'll tell ye aal an aaful story…' I guess that's how it ought to begin. Well, for all my mid-Atlantic accent, I come from around here. I was born in Westgate and went to school up-dale. The school's been shut for years. The County never thought it amounted to much, but what I learned there set me up for life. In every sense.

I had one pal, Craig. Amid those farmers' sons we stood out, not always to our credit. We were little techies, always getting hold of some dangerous gadget or other—or constructing our own.

One day Craig dared me to make a hydrogen bomb. What if it had worked, we didn't stop to consider. Which goes to show what good scientists we were, for all our tender years. But it might have been better if it had worked, because what I succeeded in making instead was something far more dreadful.

I knew there was massive pressure inside a collapsing bubble. Humble surface tension, but vastly amplified by the astronomically increasing curvature as the bubble gets smaller. I guessed maybe it was enough to trigger the hydrogen-to-helium reaction if we helped it collapse faster. Long, patient observation had shown me how to worm my way into the explosives compound at the quarry and get the hasp off the steel door. So we stole some plastic explosive and a detonator and took them down the Wear. There we fired a shaped charge wrapped round a lead pipe filled with Irn-Bru.

We hid ourselves behind the river bank, but Craig couldn't resist peeping as it went off. A fragment smacked him in the forehead and killed him outright. I ran, but I knew I couldn't just pike off without being able to say what had happened to him, so back I crept.

He was lying on his side, flung down on the ground like dirty laundry. I was too scared to touch him, but as I stared down at his motionless body, something dropped out of his face and lay smoking in the wet leaves. It was a pea-sized lump of lead. I went to pick it up but it was molten, like butter. I found a tin can to put it in and took it home. I thought it was the explosive that had made it hot, but by next morning it still hadn't cooled down.

Nobody knew I'd been there, so I sat guiltily in class whilst they said prayers for Craig, secretly rattling the lead pellet in a tube of water to keep it solid.

Then a wonderful thing happened. The pellet disgorged a tiny spark, so small it floated like a grain of dust and showed no sign of sinking. I had it with me day and night, constantly taking it out to have a look at it.

My pet star: it shone brilliantly in the dark for something so wee. I set the alarm to wake me every two hours to give the tube a shake. I didn't want it settling on the glass sides in case it went out. I developed a sore on my thigh next to my trouser pocket, and another one under my left nipple by my pyjama top pocket, but I didn't make the connection.

One day teacher saw me playing with the tube in class. She confiscated it and put it in her desk. Next morning I got a chance to sneak it back, but to my distress the mini star had gone.

Then I felt moisture. The tube was leaking through a tiny hole. I peered inside the teacher's desk. A blackened pinhole went through the class register, right through the bottom of the desk and on down through the floorboards. I put the tube back in the desk and never said a word.

*　*　*

When I left school I went to Newcastle University and studied Astrophysics, special topic: black holes. There was no decent work for physicists in England, so I crossed the pond, did my postgrad at Caltech and got a job at Lawrence Livermore National Laboratory—aka the Skunkworks. From there I joined a firm specialising in advanced weapon systems and soon became a partner. We won a series of big Federal contracts. Really big ones, let me tell you.

My life was all about making bigger and better bangs. Fuel-air was my specialty: the most powerful non-nuclear explosion you can make. In fact these things get mistaken for mini nukes like the US Army's Davy Crockett hand-launched plutonium bomb. What, never heard of it? A couple-thousand of these things

got manufactured in the late fifties. And they're not all
accounted for: which is something people choose to
forget. I got rich—the West was busy arming Saddam
Hussein and he was buying all the latest weaponry he
could get his hands on. But people were shy of selling
him nukes, and Mossad were killing anyone who tried.
So my hardware was right up his street.

Yeah, I know what you're thinking: how could I
relish getting rich on the proceeds of mass destruction?
But I told myself these mega weapons never get used.
They're there to scare people into their right minds.
That's how I squared my conscience.

And boy—did I sleep at nights! I had a villa at
Santa Barbara and another in Monterey overlooking
the beach. I had penthouse studios in San Francisco
and Hollywood, plus holiday shacks all over the place,
Weed, Boca, Seattle, Niagara Falls, Martha's
Vineyard... from which you'll gather my sideline was
real estate.

I had my pick of the women too. At weekends,
with the latest girlfriend, I'd take my Learjet and go
skiing and scuba diving all over the Union.

One day I attended a top-secret presentation by a
one-armed guy from Yorktown Heights—the IBM
research laboratory in upstate New York. His topic
was Applied Gravitation. Nothing to thrill you,
perhaps. But to an astrophysicist it's like saying
Applied Astronomy. Applied Supernovas. Applied
Stellar Creation and Destruction. Now I understood

why IBM was rumoured to be, oh-so-reluctantly, in the mega weapons business.

A black hole forms naturally in the centre of a star more than 2.5 times the mass of the sun, because that's when gravitational pressure at the core overcomes the so-called Strong Force, the last barrier holding matter apart, and it collapses to nothingness. Did you know that something has to be holding matter apart? That the energy you'd recover by letting it all fall in on itself from the furthest star is equal to the energy in the universe locked up in matter itself? By Mach's Principle the two balance out, so the total energy of the entire universe is zero.

Zero! Zilch! *Nishto!* The entire universe, with its space-time, its energy, its matter, has all been dragged out of nothing! And a black hole is simply the universe going back to nothing.

Now I've mentioned stars bigger than 2.5 solar masses. For a long while people thought it meant black holes couldn't come any smaller. Unless, like Stephen Hawking, you believed in the existence of mini black holes. But this guy said he didn't need to believe: he *knew.* How? He'd made one in the laboratory.

Someone asked him from the floor how he had contained it. 'Just wouldn't you like to know,' he replied. 'But let me tell you: if I'd let that critter get away, it would have sunk to the center of the Earth. And in two hundred years the whole shebang would've collapsed like an eggshell.'

In that instant my peace of mind blew away forever.

I followed Chuck, the gravity guru, back to the bar and tried to find out just how he'd made his black hole. He said that was classified information: why did I want to know? So I told him what I had done as a boy, down by the banks of the river Wear.

His eyes crinkled in a paternal sort of way. 'Why, that's impossible. How could you could have induced a Schwarzschild singularity with the puny pressures you had access to? Gelignite, you say? Soda water? Can you guess what I had to use?' He shook his head slowly. '*Impossible!*'

'*Impossible* is not a quantum-mechanical concept,' I mumbled.

A bark of mirth. He squared up to me with his good fist as if I were a four-year-old that had just landed him a punch.

'You know? You're right! Not impossible. Just *vanishingly improbable!*'

He unclenched his fist. 'So you reckon it tunnelled?'

I nodded.

'Okay—what colour was it?'

'Deep mauve, like a sunbed. But grainy as you moved your head, like a tiny laser. The light seemed to come from far, far away.'

The patronising smile faded to blankness, and then to creeping horror. Lunging for the bar phone, he stabbed out a number.

'Hedda? Book me two seats on the next flight to England!'

* * *

Twelve hours later, Chuck and I were in Ireshopeburn, kicking over the ashes of my old school. It had burned down only weeks before, they told us. Prior to that, the building had been sealed for years with heavy boards over the doors and windows and the power had been off all that time. The blame was put on vandals, but the barman wondered who'd have wanted to be out that night because it had been blowing a blizzard.

By daylight there was nothing to see, so we toured the pubs in St. John's Chapel, questioning the natives.

But when we went back after dark… oh boy!

It was a quiet night, with a chill mist rising from the meadows. By torchlight we crept down the blackened stone steps into what was left of the cellar and began to turn the rubbish over, without much hope of finding anything. Suddenly my foot dislodged some debris and Chuck wrenched me backwards with a shout. A mauve flame, needle thin, lanced straight up in front of my forehead, almost parting my hair. We both stared at it going up and up in the misty air like a shining thread. Chuck held out a charred slat, I smelt the dry smoke of old wood and the tip clattered onto broken slates.

'That's Hawking radiation!' howled Chuck. 'Do you know what you've done?'

113

I didn't answer. I just stared back at him.

'You've done lost me the Nobel Prize!'

*   *   *

Chuck said he didn't need me: he knew what to do. So back I went to California and got on with my life. I thought thank God it wasn't my problem. Then one night, two years later, I had a visit from a guy calling himself Rodriguez who flashed me his ID. I recognised the sixteen-point star of the CIA.

He took out a forty-five. I said 'Hey, I'm just about to meet my girlfriend!'

'No you're not. You're about to go on a long trip with me.'

'Where to?'

'To Weardale, UK.'

I felt like I'd swallowed a hot potato. I said 'Lemme phone Mary-Beth… *please!*'

'No way. You've just dropped through a hole in the ground.'

*   *   *

So back to Weardale I went. This time it wasn't by scheduled flight, but in the cavernous belly of a US Airforce Hercules with nil formalities. The Dale looked as lovely as ever, but it gave me no pleasure. Instead of checking into a pub, as Chuck and I had done, Rodriguez drove the CD-plated Range Rover up

114

a bumpy track which led nowhere except to one of the derelict cottages dotted about on the fell. With his handgun he motioned me out.

I was sure I was going to be wasted. But why bring me all this way to do it? As I stood against the wall of the cottage, Rodriguez pointed a remote control and there was a hiss behind me. A chamber opened in the wall like a metal-lined coffin. Rodriguez signed to me to step back into it and the lid hissed shut and I dropped like I was on a bungee line. The coffin lid opened and I was in a brightly-lit bunker, surrounded by guards looking like US marines, but with no insignias I knew. Another hiss and Rodriguez emerged behind me. The guards saluted.

'Welcome to Earthspot Zero,' he said to me in a flat voice. 'Let me show you to your room. I'm afraid you'll have me for company tonight.'

A bottle of scotch and two glasses stood on the table. Boy, I needed that drink. Even after three stiff measures each, Rodriguez still kept one hand on the forty-five. He hadn't let me out of his sight for an instant.

Half an hour later Chuck burst in. He levelled his finger at me.

'At this moment in time, your black hole is six miles down—and still going! Once it's through the earth's crust there'll be no getting it back.' He turned to Rodriguez, 'So you turkeys better come up with a sensible plan to raise it—and fast!'

'We're doing all we can,' Rodriguez snapped back. 'Congress needs to be kept in the dark. And so—by God—do the Brits.'

They then both stared at me as if I'd just unilaterally declared the Third World War. I felt I ought to say something.

'Aren't you getting any cooperation from the British Government?'

'Oh, they know we're here. But how many of us— and what we're planning to do—that's something they don't know.'

'It's all a big secret?'

Rodriguez shrugged. 'They're dead against it. The UK Chief Scientist says it'll be impossible to contain and it will waste the land from Edinburgh to Leeds. However they're delighted if we want to exploit its energy output, seeing as it promises to slow its descent. The official line is: nothing's going to happen for 200 years, so let's make the most of it.'

'And then the earth dissolves in a fireball!' shouted Chuck. 'Whatever are they thinking of?'

'The next election...' groaned Rodriguez.

I said 'What do you mean: exploit its energy output?'

Chuck turned to me and opened his palm. 'The Brits think we're in the geothermal business. We're here at their invitation—it's a $15 billion contract. Currently your black hole is supplying the UK National Grid with approximately one third of all its power. But that's less than point-one percent of the total energy we're having to drain off and—well—lose. That amounts to serious energy pollution if we were to let it all out on the surface of the earth. So we're beaming it off into space!'

'This,' said Rodriguez, 'is a covert operation against a friendly power. The geothermal contract's just peanuts: we're getting all the resources we need from the USA. But if the Brits get wise, the President disowns us. Right now we've gotten two thousand military personnel hidden below ground and a Titan IV in a silo the size of an oil rig—all brought in under cover of this massive energy contract. The plan to date is to raise the black hole, cram it in the rocket and fire it into deep space.'

'Deep space!' I croaked. 'Out of the solar system...?'

'We don't want it coming back round again like a comet,' said Chuck. 'Not even in ten thousand years. We don't want it in the sun neither. What would *you* do with it?'

'We *know* what he'd do with it,' snarled Rodriguez. 'What he did with it. Fucked off and forgot about it.'

*　　*　　*

The black hole was still no bigger than a blood cell. A *blood cell!* But growing all the time. It was hot enough as it sank through the earth to melt a cavity far greater than its Schwarzschild Radius. A cavity which grew wider the more matter it swallowed, forming a near-perfect cone whose base was now a sea of lava a quarter-mile across. Sunk in that dreadful sea, the black hole sucked in lava and sweated off a tenth of the mass as heat, light and gamma radiation. Everyone called it the Worm.

I said to Chuck 'If we could hit it with something, mightn't it just distort and implode?'

'We've tried all that,' he replied. 'The Worm wins every time. It's superintelligent.'

'*Superintelligent?*' I gargled. 'Did I hear you right? How can something elemental like a black hole be *superintelligent?*'

'In the same way that fire can be alive', explained Chuck. 'Doesn't fire grow, feed, move, breathe oxygen...?'

'Yes but—that's just a misuse of language! Life... Intelligence... why they're...'

'What does it matter what they are?' snapped Rodriguez. 'The net result is the same. You end up savaged by a wild beast which is a whole lot smarter than you are.'

Chuck was a little more patient with me. 'Ask yourself: what is intelligence but the capacity to guess the future, plus the will to do something about it? Just so with black holes.' He pointed his one and only forefinger downwards in front of my nose. 'As you go down through a black hole, you don't just travel along relativistically-dilatated distance. You also travel back through dilatated time, right back to the moment it was created. Now the Big Bang embraces all of space-time in our universe. But a black hole is actually a little Big Bang: inside its event horizon it has its own private space-time manifold. And this, as Einstein showed for the macro universe, is closed yet unbounded: a hypersphere.'

Inside my head the light went on. But I didn't like what I saw. 'You mean since it was created by an act of my will, only by an act of my will can it be destroyed?'

'Exactly! The two key ingredients of intelligence are Prediction and Will. The predictability of a closed time loop (a geodesic in its local space-time), plus *your* will. Knowing the exact time of its own destruction, it defeats all prior attempts. It cannot do anything else without violating the Principle of Causality, General Relativity, space-time connectedness—anything else you care to name. Hence the *illusion*—and I stress the word—of invincible intelligence.'

Rodriguez chuckled without amusement. 'Intelligence, Jim, but not as we know it.'

'So this is what you've dragged me all the way from California for?'

Chuck smiled. 'I was wrong to let you go back there. I didn't realise it until the Worm started playing its tricks—and I did a few calculations to find out why.'

'What if I don't destroy it?'

'Then the end of *its* world is coterminous with the end of ours. We all meet up on Judgement Day. And that won't be too long coming.'

                    *   *   *

They took me to the canteen and we collected trays of
food. There was a private dining room for high-
ranking officers. There Chuck told me how he had
created his black hole, a tiny spark like mine. It had
escaped from its containment vessel and dropped
through a crack in the laboratory floor. They'd brought
in a digger and dug down yards. But whenever they
caught up with it, it would melt into the subsoil like a
flea in a dog's coat.

'But when I went down the hole, it recognised me
as its Creator… and Destroyer,' said Chuck. 'It came
to my hand.'

'How cute,' I observed sourly.

'And I simply snuffed it out with my thumb and
forefinger.'

'And I bet it hardly left a mark on your skin!' I was
thinking how my black hole wasn't a pretty little spark
anymore: it was a giga-megawatt furnace. But the
words were scarcely out of my mouth when my eye fell
on Chuck's empty sleeve.

He saw me looking and he gave me that crinkle-
eyed paternal gaze before turning his face aside. 'I was
planning on doing the job myself. But General
Relativity—or the Law of Karma—says it's got to be
you.'

'How the hell do I get down there,' I muttered,
'without smashing to pieces at the bottom? Or do I
just go plop in the lava?'

Chuck took a deep breath. 'We've filled the pit with water. It's not a pit any longer: it's a well.'

'What's the point of that?'

'It drains off the Worm's power by cooling the surrounding rock, so slowing its descent. It shields the harmful radiation… and it lets us float things down.'

'Perhaps the Brits are right. If we can halt its descent or slow it right down, maybe that's all we need to do…'

'Dream on, son! As fast as we're pouring in water, the Worm's boiling it away! It's drawing ahead of our capacity to quench it. In the end of course it's bound to.'

He got up and strolled around the table. 'The water's at boiling point, even at the top here. At the bottom, God only knows what it is: a state of matter not encountered on the surface of the earth. We're sending you down in a refrigerated craft.'

'You're the bait,' said Rodriguez, grimacing in mock sympathy at my sagging jaw. 'You lure it up and we'll cram it in the space rocket.'

I glanced wild-eyed from one to the other. Chuck sighed and dropped his head. Rodriguez stared at his nails.

*   *   *

Next day Rodriguez took me by underground moving walkway to the derelict mine just up the road from my old school. What I saw made my blood run cold.

Nothing was visible on the surface, nothing out of the ordinary, but underground there had been recent mining activity—on a prodigious scale.

A shaft had been sunk two thousand feet, at which level the Worm's conical well had widened from its original pinhole to some forty feet across. We put on hard hats and entered the cage and a concealed pit wheel dropped us like a stone. The air grew hot. We walked the length of a gallery to a reinforced window looking into the Worm's well. Beside the window, water tumbled from a wide adit cut through the wall of the well and went thundering down another five hundred feet into boiling foam.

On a word from Rodriguez the spotlights on this subterranean Niagara were switched off. A mauve glow like a sunbed crept up from the depths of the pit and glittered off the glassy black walls—solid bedrock which the Worm sinking past had melted into obsidian.

Now this may come as a surprise, but a black hole ain't black. It shines brightly with Hawking radiation. There's also Cherenkov radiation: the shockwaves from highly energetic particles travelling in a refractive medium. The result was bright enough to seep up through six miles of muddy water.

Dangling on chains over this witch pot was the refrigerated craft Chuck had mentioned. Imagine a short fat gas cylinder with two bulging portholes like googly eyes, laced about with thick scaffolding from which hung a collection of bizarre gizmos, notably two massive lobster claws on jointed arms. I struggled to recall where I had ever seen anything like it before. That is, with waking eyes.

But it wasn't all unfamiliar. Slung beneath it like a monstrous penis was a finned projectile. I didn't need telling what *that* was—I'd seen one at an armaments show. The BFT-5 Thermonuclear Torpedo: the most destructive marine weapon ever devised.

A magnificent weapon, if you have the luxury of forty or fifty sea miles between you and your target. But in the confines of that well the guy who squeezed the trigger would die.

Spectacularly!

'Meet Pierre and Marcel from the *Institut Cousteau.*' Marcel stuck his Gauloise to his lower lip and held out a hand as rough as pumice stone. Pierre just nodded.

'That's their vessel, the cryothermo-bathyscaphe— CTB for short. It is built to withstand the pressures encountered at a depth of six miles. Its cryomagnetic shield will keep you cool for the duration of the dive.'

'Where's all the water coming from?'

'The adit you can see opposite has been driven through solid rock to the bottom of Derwent Reservoir. As you may know the reservoir is three miles wide. We need fresh water. Sea water won't do— when superheated it releases vast quantities of poisonous halogens. Right now we're driving another adit through to Kielder Water—sixty miles to the north-west and the largest artificial reservoir in Britain. The water from there will last us a little longer.'

'What does the water company say to all this?' I gasped.

'We own the water company. We bought it up on the open market. We'll carry on bellyaching to customers about what dry winters we've been having.'

Back in our room at the dormitory bunker I freaked out. I walked round in front of Rodriguez and shook my fingernails in his face. 'I've seen everything! I've had enough!'

Rodriguez didn't answer. He was sitting shredding a match.

'I'm going back to California! You can't keep me here! You can't make me do this thing!'

Still he didn't say a word. I continued to rage at him. 'Nothing's going to happen in our lifetime—so why should I worry? Why should *you*, for that matter?'

'Listen,' he said quietly. 'I've spent my career propping up rotten little dictators, kicking nice guys in the teeth, because somebody thought it was good for the USA. But this time I'm not doing it for Uncle Sam…'

'That's something I never thought to hear from a CIA man!'

'It's all for the healing of Mother Earth.'

He rose to his feet and stared me in the face. His eyes held a sort of pious awe. 'The question you want to ask yourself is: are you a natural-born son of the Earth? Or a goddam *motherfucker*?'

* * *

'Now remember: you're not the only person here who's scared. They're all frightened boys in there. They're a long way from home and not sure when they'll be getting back—if ever. They're living day and night below ground because they aren't supposed to be here. We can't let them out to sit in the pubs and complain there's no ice and the glasses aren't chilled without our cover being blown. This ain't what they signed up for. But they're ready to go through with it, every one.'

I followed Rodriguez in. A thousand men rose silently and stood to attention.

Chuck was at the podium. The entire personnel of Earthspot Zero were being briefed in two shifts. There was not a sound as he spoke. He explained why they were here—to enable Operation Earthspot to be completed in case London tried to stop us, which it surely would, if it knew we were planning to raise the Worm. If the Brits attacked there would be no reinforcements—and no prisoners taken. The President would disclaim all knowledge of us. Earthspot Zero would cease to exist—and would never have done so.

But the real enemy was not London, nor the British Government: it was directly beneath our feet. Implacable enemy of Great Britain, of the USA, of the whole earth, for all future generations. Our mission was to make it possible there might just be future generations.

Chuck outlined the options and the fall-back plans. The Worm mostly stayed at the bottom of the well. But it could move. And it could almost certainly be lured to the surface. Everything had to be geared to the Titan IV countdown, which was due to start at midnight.

At lift-off minus one hour, the CTB, manned by a single volunteer, would commence its dive. It had grabs—which might work or they might not. It had tokamaks: plasma bottles with superconducting magnets—which might immobilise the Worm for precious seconds, even though nothing could contain it for long. One way or another it would be lured, coaxed or corralled to the surface into a specially constructed gallery and steam blasted, together with the CTB and its occupant, into the Titan IV rocket, to take it away from the planet for ever.

How long could the rocket be expected to contain the Worm? It had only to accelerate its passenger to escape velocity. Even if the Worm burned its way out (as it surely would) by then it would be launched on a trajectory out of the solar system.

And if all else failed, the CTB carried a thermonuclear torpedo. Which might succeed in destroying the Worm—or it might not. Hopefully we wouldn't have to put it to the test.

He didn't mention our biggest worry—a question of fundamental cosmology, plus elementary physics. How much did a black hole weigh that had swallowed a billion tons of rock? Opinion differed. Some physicists said a billion tons—simple as that. Others said no: viewed from this side of the event horizon the mass was in free fall towards the singularity at the centre of the black hole. And would forever remain so.

I'd put it to Chuck. 'The Titan IV is the world's biggest skyhook. But it can't lift a billion tons. It's just gonna sit there blazing away in its silo, going nowhere!'

Chuck replied 'Look. For all its enormous mass, the Worm can move about. How?—I don't know. Some relativistic effect of a singularity in quasi-Euclidean space. But move about it does—and it can move damn fast. We've discovered *that* by bitter experience.'

'Are you trying to tell me that to get the Worm off the planet we need its *cooperation?*'

Chuck eyed me with his head down. 'The Worm's fate is quantum-entangled with yours. Once you invite it to do so, the Worm will follow you to the world's end. To get it off the planet we don't need to accelerate a billion tons… we only need to accelerate *you*!'

*   *   *

'Are there any questions?' Chuck asked the audience, trying to sound both confident and discouraging. I expected a flurry of hands, but there was silence. Two rows back, a black marine, a fresh faced boy with shining eyes who'd have looked better in baseball gear, raised his hand. 'Sir! Will you be calling for a volunteer to go down in the CTB, Sir?' The men around him groaned.

I sank in my seat for shame. Here was I, shitting myself to be out of Earthspot Zero and back home in California. This man had heard everything Chuck had had to say, yet he was eager to go down in my place.

'No, soldier,' Chuck replied. 'The volunteer has been chosen.' Turning to me he held out his one remaining arm. 'Here is the volunteer who will go down in the CTB! A big hand, you guys!'

Rodriguez pushed me to my feet and began clapping vigorously.

Without any further prompting, the audience stood as one man and cheered. Cold sweat ran down inside my shirt. Never could such heroic acclaim have been accorded to such a snivelling coward.

*   *   *

On the stroke of midnight, the public address boomed out 'Lift-off minus seventy-two hours!' My water froze: the Titan IV countdown had begun. The careful drills of the last two years swung into action for real. From that moment, the time to lift-off was announced at quarter-hour intervals. Each time my stomach went into spasm and my forehead broke out in a cold sweat.

Taking advantage of my newfound popularity, I wandered innocently up to the south gate and chatted to the guard on duty. The gate was well camouflaged and we could see without being seen. And I could see

128

soldiers. Thousands of them. There were troop carriers and armoured vehicles drawn up all along the road. Sandbagged positions were being hastily erected. All the attention and weaponry was clearly being directed at us.

'What's going on, soldier?'

'They've found out what we're up to, sir. And they're damned if they aren't gonna stop us. They've sealed off the whole of Earthspot Zero—no one's leaving here today. There's been no communication with the silo complex for over an hour. There's a rumour the SAS have overrun it.'

The guard put two cigarettes in his mouth, lit them both and gave me one. I weighed up my chances of making a bolt for it. I was hoping the besiegers might give me covering fire, like Checkpoint Charlie, but more likely my friendly guard would have shot me in the back or the Brits would have shot me in the chest as I ran towards them. But anything was better than being crushed below ground like a cockroach when the boot came down.

As I was trying to summon the courage to scramble up and run, a frail old man came hobbling towards us on sticks. It was my dad! They must have let him out of his home, or he'd absconded again—he was always doing that.

'Hallo, my boy,' he said when he spotted me. 'They told me you were back in England and I guessed here was where you were, so I thought I'd drop in to see you.'

'How the hell did you get past the soldiers?'

'Oh, I told them I'd got a son in there and they made no trouble.'

'Christ, dad! This is the last place on earth I ever, ever wanted to see you!'

'Give over, lad! Family comes first, I say. I thought you'd like a bit of moral support.'

Just then the guard turned and screamed at us, 'Get back inside! They're attacking!'

As he was speaking, half a mile away the fell erupted in a thunderous roar. A vast black fountain arose and suddenly blazed out like the sun. The carcass of the Titan IV rose upwards like a leaping whale and collapsed back in a churning froth of lox and flaming kerosene. Stones and rocks began pattering down around us. I grabbed my old dad and bundled him into the coffin-sized elevator. In less than a minute we were in the control room and they sat him down and fed him coffee and donuts.

And there I had to leave him to die when the SAS stormed the complex. Rodriguez grabbed my arm and we dropped down the pit shaft to the CTB.

'We must get you deep enough before the Brits can depth charge you.'

I tried to speak, but nothing came out. I tried again. 'It's all over! What can we do against the Worm now?'

'The Titan IV's out of the reckoning, but you've still got your thermonuclear torpedo.'

I swallowed hard. 'And you?'

'Orders are to resist to the last man. Anyhow they tell us the Brits are taking no prisoners.'

'How will the President explain to Congress the total disappearance of two thousand serving personnel?'

'That's his problem, not yours. Your job is to get down there and battle it out with the Worm.'

He held out his hand. 'So long, and good luck. I guess we won't be seeing each other again.'

*　　*　　*

I scrambled in. The hatch clanged shut and was hurriedly bolted down with power spanners. The cryo units began to hum and the air grew chill, my panting breath making fist-shaped clouds. Massive valves deep in the rock slowly shut off the cascade thundering from the Derwent adit. In the steamy spotlights the CTB began to creak slowly down from its gantry. I watched the greasy bubbling stew welling up around the portholes. A clang and a lurch as the hook disengaged. Then I was dropping like a cannonball down a boiling well, deeper than the deepest ocean rift.

Battle was raging in the bunkers of Earthspot Zero. I could picture Rodriguez holding off SAS troops in the gallery with his forty-five, as they abseiled down the pit shaft. Chuck, with an Uzi on his one good arm, in a last desperate stand. Soon there would be nobody alive who knew I was there, let alone what I was supposed to be doing.

131

I was sinking down a deep, deep well, in superheated water, or something denser than water which is steam at benthic pressures. At the bottom, in extreme conditions, I would come face-to-face with the most devastating horror you can imagine: a superintelligent dragon gulping down the earth.

And all because of a schoolboy dare.

The livid glow grew brighter and brighter, glaring through the portholes of the CTB, until I could see them as clear as day even with my eyes shut. Then I saw the Worm. It rose from its molten lake in a huge swan neck of glowing lava, shedding droplets in a trail. It reared up to meet me, to swallow me and crush me to nothing: the first of six billion victims.

I fired the thermonuclear torpedo.

It missed!

The Worm spread out like my fingers. Virtual images, of course—but no telling which was the real one. As the torpedo slipped off into the distance the Worm, now a naked point of infinite brilliance, probed and bumped the steel scaffold surrounding the CTB, snipping off grabs and bottles like pruning a shrub. Suddenly with a screech and a roar it fastened to the side of the pressure vessel. The cryomagnetic shield collapsed. Everything began to plunge down the shining throat.

Just at that instant the torpedo, describing a wide circle, came back and found its target. We were so deep underground the tremor would only just have rattled the glasses up here. But the cryothermo-bathyscaphe was instantly annihilated.

*　　*　　*

From the look in your eyes I know just what you're thinking. How can anyone *know* what goes on in the dead centre of a thermonuclear blast, in a confined space, when the very centre is itself a black hole?

Well, I can't enlighten you all that much. I can only say: macro-quantum effects. The Laws of Physics were momentarily suspended. For a femtosecond I *was* the Worm. The Worm had been me all along. In that instant I was All-Knowing! All-Powerful!

I chose to live. And to let the Earth live.

But as I was projected out through spheres of mortality, I knew it would all come to the same in the end. The contents of the Derwent Adit are now lumps of ice tumbling through space, but I materialised a mere two thousand feet up. Any higher and I'd have stifled in the thin air. Any lower and I'd have been smashed to pieces by flying rocks. Omnipotence gauges to a whisker.

And would you believe it! Bound for the bottom of a six-mile well, facing conditions never before experienced by man, it occurred to someone I'd might just need a parachute! I came down nearby and realised this was Blanchland. So I walked down the hill to the Lord Crewe Arms... and here we are.

133

Am I all right, did you say? Oh yes—for the present. When I was all-powerful, I should have remembered the effects of intense radiation. But it slipped my mind. Nothing seems to happen at first, then your bodily functions pack up. I ought to check myself into hospital, but what's the use? I guess I'll just take a stroll round Derwent Reservoir, what's left of it, and see the sun go down.

So… thanks for the drink. Enjoy the rest of your wedding party. I'm so glad your daughter got off safely. California, was it? Nice. Tell her to blow it a kiss from me.

FACE 48

*'Ye shall meet and remember, and love them
again.'*
(Gardner & Valiente: The Book of Shadows)

'It was a long time ago,' said the little old nun with cheeks like walnuts. 'Such a long time… Over the years I have come to the realisation that the experience was—how do you say in English?—a *symbol.*'

She sorted doubtfully through the pile of cards. 'I do not mean it did not really happen. Oh yes, it happened. For me—it happened. But there are levels of reality. Faces… these must belong to the lowest level.'

She had a point. I was beginning to feel stupid. Why hadn't I chosen a nice safe project on the inner-city environment or the incidence of smoking cannabis in twelve-year-old girls, like my supervisor Enid had suggested? But there were only two female part-time MSc students in a bunch of men and I was one of them. I needed to be a lot more daring.

Suddenly the old nun gaped at me. Her chin sagged. Without another word she put the card she was holding into the envelope, got up and left the room.

*　　*　　*

In a double-blind experiment, it is important that the experimenter doesn't know the subject's choice, nor even the correct answer. In that way the 'Clever Hans' effect can be controlled—the illusion of the counting horse that was responding to unconscious cues from its owner. The academic merit of my experiment, as Enid pointed out, was that there was no correct answer. At least, none that intelligent people would accept.

*　　*　　*

'I know what Fisher would have said. "So little data…"' Enid held me in her gaze, wincing ever so slightly. To reinforce her academic credibility she affected this nervous tic, so that people wouldn't fixate on how stunningly beautiful she was. "'…But so little variance, one is impressed by the strength of the signal." It's certainly not the outcome I expected.'

'Two subjects chose the same picture. As for the pictures chosen by the other two subjects… well, one old dear could hardly see! But they're both ones which resemble Face 48…'

I was sorry the moment I said it. Enid pounced on it straight away. 'What do you mean, 'resemble'? You can't write that in a dissertation. It betrays a deep misunderstanding of the experimental method. You must employ some objective measure of resemblance between two given faces.'

136

I must have looked doubtful. 'What about the generation parameters?' she persisted.

'They don't correlate significantly with what people *perceive* as facial resemblance.'

Enid pouted. 'Then you have a problem.'

But I also had an answer. 'I got my fellow students to sort the pictures into piles. Running the results against MDSCAL gave me a space of ninety-nine dimensions.' I bubbled like a gleeful child. 'Here, I've plotted the two principal components which account for 83% of the variance as x and y axes…'

How I lusted after her approval in everything I did!

I scrabbled through my briefcase and handed her a sheet. 'A scatterplot. How interesting.' I thought she was being dismissive, but she wasn't.

'There's a point for every picture. They're all numbered. I've used orange marker on number 48 and the other two. The contours are not my idea of a cluster—they're the computer's…'

'Yes, yes, I can see that.' Enid's impatience showed she was excited. She pored over the sheet in silence, then she said, 'There's no doubt about it, they *are* tightly clustered.'

She handed the sheet back to me with a smile. 'The results are good. Almost too good. If we were in a court of law (and thank heavens we're not!)—you'd have no difficulty convincing the jury that all four witnesses saw the same person. Every day people go to prison on far weaker evidence.'

She screwed up her eyes and shook her head as if she was trying to shake off a monkey hanging on her lovely blonde hair. 'But scientifically the whole idea's preposterous!'

'The external examiner isn't going to like it, is he? I had hoped for greater variance, then it would all pass off as just a training in methodology...' I faltered as she made a Martian face at me.

'So what am I to do?' I pleaded.

'Stop worrying. I've nothing but admiration for the way you've persisted in gaining access to these people. I've seen your collection of letters with flying buttresses and fancy hats—I hope you're going to attach them as an appendix. Just apply the statistics correctly and draw the right conclusions, and you'll be OK.'

The clock struck two. I got up to go.

'Oh... non-parametric, mind! You can't assume underlying normality...'

Her voice tailed off. Can't assume underlying normality! It was as if she were looking to me for reassurance rather than the other way round.

'What's the likelihood of the outcome occurring by chance? You must have worked that out.'

'Approximately one in four hundred and thirty million.'

She swallowed. 'Well... a year or so back a man was struck by lightning on the Downs. His shooting stick was melted to the seat of his pants, but he lived.

Probability of that happening's got to be something of the same order of magnitude…'

*   *   *

I had Face 48 blown up and framed. I hung it in my bathroom and spent hours sitting there just looking at it. I wondered if I ought to pray to it. For a computer-generated face it was surprisingly realistic. One hundred pictures, spanning a subspace of facial characteristics. By definition, each one was a picture of nobody at all. But everybody who had ever been born must resemble one or other of the pictures to some degree. Of course if Jason had generated me an ensemble of all possible racial types and hairstyles, the pictures would have run to millions, but we felt safe sticking to a sub-selection—young, female, Jewish. We replaced the undefined hairstyle in every picture by the same stylised blue veil.

So what was so special about Face 48? It was nothing out of the ordinary, neither plain nor all that beautiful. It was memorable, yes, but out of those hundred pictures it wasn't one of the top ten I'd have chosen as the image of the Virgin Mary.

*   *   *

I graduated with distinction—in spite of the examiners' reservations about Marian apparitions as a fit topic for an MSc dissertation. My first job was in

139

West Hartlepool and it gave me no time to go thinking through the implications of my research. I ended each day frayed and exhausted.

My job was interviewing a succession of disturbed teenagers from appalling backgrounds. Three quarters had been abused in childhood—often by stepfather or elder brother. Pregnancies and abortions had been the rule, not once, but several times. Most had experimented with solvents or drugs by the age of nine. But just as I thought I had seen it all, Melanie walked into my life.

I'd studied her file, so I pretended to myself I was ready for anything, but the instant I set eyes on her a thunderbolt fused me to my swivel chair.

She was Face 48! Straight out of the picture frame and into my office. Standing there looking at me.

'OK gimme the crap,' she said.

But I could not 'give her the crap'. I was struck dumb. I was supposed to be the authoritative figure and she the submissive one, allowing for a little residual rebelliousness. She stood and smouldered at my silence, then a glimmer of something else— amusement—showed in her eyes.

'Shit, another bloody dyke,' she spat. 'Well now, *sister*, what can I do for you?'

I found my voice, kind of. 'Won't you sit down?' I said huskily.

I must have seemed like the disturbed one in that interview. Melanie talked in a flat voice, completely in control. Like a spirited horse with an inexperienced rider, she was cooperating because it was her pleasure to do so. At any moment she could have thrown me off and bolted. She walked out without looking back, her head held high as if she didn't care a toss if we never saw each other again.

Which just goes to show how wrong first impressions can be.

About 2 a.m. the following night I was called out of bed to drive through freezing fog to Winterton, the mental hospital near Trimdon. Melanie had been admitted c/o the police in a frenzied condition, high on some concoction that the staff were getting ready to stomach-pump her for. Where she got the strength from I don't know, but it took four nursing assistants to hold her down. The reek of rotten apples signalled that paraldehyde (50cc, intramuscular)—we called it 'chemical cosh'—had already been added to the witches' brew coursing round her bloodstream.

The treatment room was wrecked. She had been screaming for me and, on being told she couldn't just call for someone she'd only met once and expect them to come running, she promised to take the ward apart, screw by screw.

Now Winterton had plenty of experience with that sort of thing, but in this case they judged it expedient to ring my flat and ask if I recalled the young lady in question. Did I recall her! If I didn't, it was the last opportunity I'd ever be offered to forget her.

They told me afterwards that no sooner had she heard my voice in the corridor than all the fight went out of her and she went as floppy as a rag doll. We talked quietly for what must have been hours, because it was nearly five when I crawled back into bed. Not that it mattered because I didn't sleep. Nor the next night. My mind was buzzing.

Nobody asked me, they simply added her to my already brimming caseload. Just about every agency in County Durham and Cleveland knew Melanie, but nobody was that eager to help me out with her.

Not that she was any trouble, face to face. The endless trouble she caused me was always when I wasn't there. They told me I was the only person she addressed in anything like a civil manner, in any tone of voice but a scream. But with me she was invariably quiet and reflective.

*   *   *

It was impossible to keep my private life secure—she found out my home address all by herself. Almost the first thing she said when she had completed her inspection of my flat was, 'Why do you have a picture of me in your loo?'—spoken in a bored voice.

I thought, dare I give her the true answer? Or a plausible one? I cravenly opted for the latter. In the same bored voice I said 'So I don't have to keep going in the bedroom for a bit of a wank.'

She sniffed, as if that was my problem, not hers.

At that time doctors had no qualms about slapping the label 'schizophrenic' on people and doping them

142

with sedatives like Luminal to bring the condition
under control. But with Melanie there really wasn't any
condition to control. I found her observant, critical
(oh, so critical!)—but she was as likely to criticise her
own behaviour as that of other people. Just as if she
were another person, another perverse, inexplicable
thing in her perverse, inexplicable world.

But *person* was the wrong word to use of her. She
would make use of three or four personae, often
referring to herself as 'that monkey'. But she wasn't a
'person' in any meaningful sense of the word. She was
a convergence of sensation, a critical agency, but an
agent without an author. Perceptive, intelligent,
brilliant even, she was sensing—but not sensible.
Responding—but not responsible. Aware—but not
conscious.

I began to think of her as the Golem—the living
clay doll in Hebrew legend that lacked a soul, because
God hadn't made it, but a learned rabbi. One day, it
occurred to me with a shock that she might be
computer generated.

Yet she had battened onto me in a way I was
powerless to shift. She must have seen something in
me she needed to explain herself to herself. Was it just
that I was sympathetic to her? That I was caring? No,
she didn't appreciate that. The only time she offered
me violence was when I tried to praise her faltering
achievements and tell her that she was in reality a
sensitive, intelligent woman.

*   *   *

Then something happened between us, which meant we could no longer maintain a professional relationship. But she remained a frequent visitor to my flat—she would turn up at any hour of the day or night. I asked for her to be removed from my caseload, but my boss wouldn't hear of it. 'You're the only person she's ever responded to,' he told me. But Melanie blurted out the situation to a social worker from another agency and I nearly lost my job.

I was not ashamed. I was angry. 'You refused to take her off my caseload. You told me I was the only person she responded to. Isn't it appropriate, then, not to enquire too deeply into my methods?'

My boss, a humane person when all is said and done, patiently explained that people passed though our hands all the time and nobody expected a success rate of 100%. Some people, he said, you have to let go. Some people are screwed up, some are mad, but there's a residue that are just plain worthless. It all came out in bed with Melanie that night—I was so discouraged. But she only said, in her flat impersonal way, 'So they still hang monkeys in Hartlepool?'

*   *   *

I was forbidden to see her and she stopped coming to my flat. I heard she'd got into a bad crowd. Not the normal run of alienated youth, but bad. Whether she was attracted to this particular lad because of the things he did, or whether it was she who incited him, I don't know. I guess a bit of both. But I don't believe for one moment she actually opted to be evil. Like me, she was a researcher, but unlike me, who only needed the 'right' results to gain my qualification, the answers mattered vitally to her. She needed to know the nature, the capabilities and limitations of this strange phenomenon, the interpersonal relationship. Her new friends erected a whole new dimension.

One night in Sunderland they stole a car and four of them careered down the A19 at a hundred and fifty miles an hour, straight over the Peterlee roundabout, straight into a container lorry grinding up from Middlesbrough. It was no great thing for me to be called out in the middle of the night on her account, but this time it wasn't Winterton. It was the casualty ward of Sunderland Royal Infirmary.

She recovered consciousness long enough to say a few words. I had been holding her hand for an hour or more, when I felt it tighten feebly on my fingers. Her puffy lips moved awkwardly.

'Why do you bother with me?' It was all she said. There was no sense of guilt in it, no apology. No self-pity, even. Just a profound puzzlement.

I stared at her shattered face, with pipes up her nose and fuzzy white bandages taped over blackened pits which were her eyes. Clay—that's what the Bible calls us. If we aren't hallmarked with the face of God, then we're nothing but clay. Clay which bleeds and clots and goes sooty violet and a nasty yellow when it is treated roughly. Colours you see in thunderclouds, when God is angry.

What could I say? Should I tell her the real reason, or a convincing one? I'm not an open book to myself. I could only think of what the textbooks say. From the instant you first meet somebody, your attitude to them is basically determined by their resemblance to people you have known. Nothing to do with the actual person at all. The love they enjoy, or hatred they endure, has all been earned by someone else.

But in Melanie's case it had been resemblance to a computer-generated picture, not to someone real. A person that simply did not exist and never had done. A bitmap, an ikon, a cluster in concept-space—a *symbol*.

'You reminded me of someone…' I faltered over the lie, but it didn't matter. She wasn't listening. She wasn't there anymore.

But I went ahead and said it anyway.

'Someone… I thought I was deeply in love with.'

WE DON'T COME FROM ROUND HERE

'Bye,' said Tansy. 'Thank you for having me.'

'Bye,' said Susan, waving her off. Behind her she heard her mother grumble, 'It'd be nice if Tansy's people invited Susan back to their place occasionally.'

But *that* they would never do. Tansy herself dreaded being away from the house for long. She knew that every minute out of doors she was in mortal danger. Danger of disintegration. She let herself in with her own key and switched on the reintegrator. Tubes buzzed with coloured fire and she closed her eyes, feeling the play of lights on her face.

That was better. Now she could run the bath. She dropped careful measures of different coloured liquids into the hot water streaming from the tap. There was a proper order for doing this, with the right pauses in between each measure, which she gauged by keeping her eye on the second hand of the clock above the cabinet. She didn't want to blow up the bathroom, did she now?

The clock was like no other she had ever seen. It went round the reverse way and had twenty-five hours, but these were slightly shorter ones than other people's hours, so it still managed to lose about half an hour a day against 'outside' time. All the same, she knew that it was exactly right where they came from—it was everyone else's clocks that were wrong. Sunset, on the other hand, ran to its own schedule, which was different from anybody's. So what did it really mean to be right on time?

There came the sound of Daddy unlocking his secret way into the house. Before she got into the bath he came to the bathroom door and said hallo in their private language. Billions of people spoke it, but Daddy and Barbie were the only people she knew who did, beside herself. Neither sister dared utter a word of it outside the house, not even to each other in private.

'Give me a kiss.'

She held out a wet hand and they touched three fingertips. Daddy got down a plastic board and a chinagraph pencil dangling on strings from a nail.

'You said I could take it off when I got in the bath.'

'Please yourself.' He peered at the numbers on the small pearly box she held out to him and wrote them down on the board. 'But don't forget to strap it on again as soon as you're dry.'

'I won't,' she said in a sing-song voice.

'Where's Seventh Barbie?'

'Not back from school yet. And it's her turn to make meal-ten. I'm hungry.'

'I do wish you'd walk home together.'

'But she's let out of class at a different time to me.'

*　*　*

148

They kept religiously to the five mealtimes spaced
equally round the bathroom clock, named after their
proper hour, which was marked in yellow. Meal-five,
meal-ten, and so on. This meant in practice three meals
a day, leaving out the two mealtimes when you were
asleep or at school. They arrived roughly half an hour
later each day. When a mealtime ran into bedtime it
was dropped, and they ate instead at the earlier time
which had in the meantime crept backwards out of
school time. Meal-ten was shortly due to give way to
meal-five—and Tansy looked forward to that.

Whenever they took place, meals always followed
the same pattern. Unlike her schoolmates, she and
Barbie were allowed to play with their food. They vied
with each other to smear the carbohydrate paste into
elaborate shapes, castles and helter-skelters, down
which they'd trickle purple sauce from a silvery bottle.
Then they'd race to eat it, washing it down with
nameless juices from squeezy transparent balls. After
that they'd break open the shells of the egg-like
capsules called *mgafteldji* and compare the contents.
They once tried keeping a running count from meal to
meal of the different flavours they encountered, but
they gave up at around fifty.

Daddy sat in with them, but he'd say very little
except to break up the occasional squabble and stop
them throwing *mgafteldji* at each other. He'd never eat
anything. He'd go to his room and recharge with pure
energy, which they couldn't because they'd been

reintegrated in human form. They begged and begged
to be allowed to watch, but he never let them.

'Why can't we be like you at home?'

'Because it would take too long to get you back
into little girls. Just imagine turning up at school the
next day looking like me!'

'Well—at weekends then, or during the holidays?'

'Whatever would your friends say? It's hard
enough as it is, keeping it quiet that we don't come
from round here.'

But Daddy never told them where they *did* come
from. He always sidestepped the question, or said it
was better for them not to know because they couldn't
trust a single person to keep it secret. It was something
Tansy found out all by herself.

Once in class, the teacher had asked them which
planet had a 'day'—a period of rotation—which was
the closest to the earth's. Tansy had gone to the library
and found an astronomy book for young people which
told her straightaway. Only one planet, Mars, had a
period of rotation anything like that of the earth. But it
was pretty close: 24 hours, 39 minutes and 35 seconds.

Exactly the time it took for the bathroom clock to
go full circle.

*　　*　　*

Seventh Barbie was downstairs mixing the carbopaste
by the time Tansy had got dressed. Tansy always liked
it when it was her sister's turn to make the meal,

150

because then she got the job of hosing down the eating chamber afterwards.

'Yuk! Do you *have* to make it that colour?'

'What's wrong with it? It's the colour of your spots. You make it whatever colour you like when it's your turn.'

Daddy looked in. 'Greetings, 7B. You're back. Have you got any homework?'

'Yes. We've all got to write a page about what we do when we come home from school.'

'Well, use your imagination. Make it sound like everyone else.'

*   *   *

It was the middle of the night. But it was getting up time where they came from and Daddy woke Tansy and her sister softly. Outside, in the darkness of the overgrown back garden, he had assembled their telescope.

Tansy said 'I was dreaming about Mummy.'

'But you've never seen Mummy.'

'I know. But I saw her in my dream. She was just like you, only female. She had a pair of blue eyes—and a pair of green.'

'That's… amazing.'

'You never told us what happened to Mummy.'

'It's no secret—she disintegrated. It was awful. We left it too late and Beta-3 couldn't do a thing for her.'

'Oh!'

'Now forget about Mummy. Just tell me what you see.'

Tansy peered into the telescope. 'It's… Spica, in Virgo.'

'Let Barbie have a go. What do you think, 7B?'

'Yes, it's Spica.' She wasn't really sure, but she thought it wise to agree with her sister for once. Tansy pushed her out of the way and put her eye to the eyepiece once more.

Daddy said 'Now increase the right ascension slowly.'

'…Oh, golly! What is it? I'm sure it wasn't there a week ago.'

'It wasn't. It's Mars. It moves right round the zodiac, but not evenly of course. Why not, 7B?'

'Because the earth is moving round the sun too, in the same direction. So it's like watching someone running round you when you're sitting on a roundabout.' This time she did know the answer.

'Full marks', said Daddy. 'Mars is called the Red Planet. You can see its colour clearly.'

'You know…' said Tansy out of the side of her mouth, peering with one eye screwed up, '…if you hadn't told me it was red, I'd have said it was Pantone 129.'

In the dim violet glow of the star globe, she could see her father gazing at her searchingly.

'Yes, Fifth Tansy, you're right. It *is* Pantone 129. What your friends would call a sort of orangey-beige. Don't let people tell you any different.'

It was the very next day that she found the key.

Clutching it to her chest, she resolved to try it in every keyhole in the house until she found one that it opened. Barbie was staying at school for choir practice. Daddy had warned her he'd be late back, reassuring her it wouldn't be past twenty-five o'clock. So there was no real risk of him disintegrating. Midnight on Mars, for now Tansy knew it to be, was going to occur shortly after 10 pm UTC, so she was going to be alone in the house for a couple of hours at least.

Theirs was a big rambling Georgian house, with tremendously high ceilings on the first floor and ones that got progressively lower as you went upstairs, or down. It was just right for all the equipment that Daddy had to fix up to enable them to live on Earth without disintegrating. If her friends could only see it, their eyes would pop. But no one must ever be invited back. Daddy was most insistent about that.

One by one Tansy tried the key in every keyhole in turn, starting with the lower cellar (the house had two). There were lots of rooms she and Barbie had never been in, doors which had never ever been unlocked so far as she recalled. The key didn't fit any of those. But at last, on the fifth floor landing, in a door she'd walked past so often she no longer noticed it, the key fitted the keyhole and turned. In the gloom of the top landing (the bulb had gone), she pushed the creaky door. It swung right back with a clunk.

Two glowing eyes rushed at her and something rustling smacked her full in the chest. She fell over backwards.

She lay in the doorway, heart pounding, not daring to move. But as nothing happened for a long while, ever-so-slowly she put her hand up and felt her chest. No blood: she wasn't hurt. Whatever had hit her hadn't been all that heavy. Just as slowly she crept back along the landing, towards the glow of light seeping up the stairs. The world looked safe and ordinary once more. Nothing moved—not a sound. She rushed down the stairs as fast as she could.

*   *   *

Well, she couldn't leave it at that. Whatever horrors awaited her in the mystery room, she was more afraid of Daddy finding the door open. So she fetched a big torch from the rear lobby and went back upstairs, her chest feeling tight as though it were stuffed with feathers.

Now she saw what had hit her. A 'monster' hung there on strings. It was made of empty boxes, yoghurt pots and other junk. She laughed and felt round the door jamb where the light switch normally was, found one and switched it on. The mystery room lit up. She pushed her way past the cardboard dragon.

It took her a long time to take it all in. Round three walls was waist-high shelving which served as a workbench. On it were jars and jars of various coloured liquids, with tiny bottles scattered about the bench. Some bore labels saying they were food dyes, others vitamins. There was all the equipment you'd need for making *mgafteldji*, lots of empty eggshells, a fridge full of eggs and a small electric engraver for grinding holes in the shells to blow them. There was a blender and boxes of cans of perfectly ordinary foods like tuna, spinach, corned beef and macaroni cheese. The price labels betrayed the fact that they hadn't come from Mars but from the store down the road.

There were tools and vices and soldering irons, plus 'Martian' gadgets and contraptions of every shape and size in various stages of construction, all made of cardboard, tinsel paper and balsa wood, laced with bulbs and light-emitting diodes—she recognised those from the craft and design room at school. Last of all there was a damaged head looking like Daddy's. It was hollow and made of rubber.

She must have stood in that room for half an hour or more, when suddenly she heard a noise downstairs. It was Barbie coming home from school. Hastily she locked the door and tiptoed down the stairs. She didn't say a word to her sister, because then she would have had to show her the key.

But over meal-twenty-five, which they ate when Daddy came home, she said to him, 'There's a workshop upstairs for making Martian things.'

Instantly he leapt to his feet. 'Barbie—grab hold of Tansy, she's disintegrating—her mind's nearly gone!'

Tansy struggled and kicked, but her father, with Barbie's help, hung onto her unshakeably. 'Beta-3 will put her together again but we must be quick. Hurry!'

They dragged her upstairs, right to the secret workshop, where her father produced a key to unlock the door. He bundled her inside and locked it again. Ear to the door, she heard him telling Barbie to go downstairs and shut herself in the bathroom and wait for him to come and say it was all right, while he worked Beta-3. 'Don't cry, now. Everything will be all right. I think we've caught her in time...'

She heard a key being fumbled and dropped on the floor. In her blouse pocket Tansy still had the key she'd found. It occurred to her to put it in the lock on her side and give it a half-turn to stop it being pushed out. She could hear her father's voice imploring her, but she didn't stay to listen to what he was saying. She lifted the blind and somehow got the sash window open.

Outside the window, the Georgian facade formed a narrow balcony with the slates of the shallow sloping roof. Her mind quite numb, she crawled along it onto the next building, down a fire escape and away.

BAD STAR

'Do you suppose that's our downpour coming?' said the stalky old man. On one of the ten days of witch camp there'd always be a cloudburst. It had become something of a tradition: we'd all tear our clothes off and dance naked in the rain.

Shading my eyes to peer at the horizon, I shook my head. 'Looks too small to be a rain cloud.'

'Well,' said the old man in a testy voice, 'it's the one I ordered.'

Seeing the look on my face, his features softened. 'Haha. Just joking.'

But he wasn't, you know.

Within the hour we had the biggest rainstorm I'd ever been caught in. But the old man wasn't enjoying it. He was running round in the marquee with a broom, tipping out the bulges of rainwater swelling on the slanting roof to stop the canvas ripping. I found another broom and went to help him.

Outside the entrance a trio of girls danced in the sopping grass, flinging their arms wide and twirling on their toes in the mud. One of them was called Chris: she looked so exuberant and beautiful, her red hair streaming in rivulets down her milk-white skin.

A lightning flash lit up the field. At that very instant I made a wish, knowing that it couldn't help but come true. How I wish I'd wished for something else! But at the time I didn't have a choice.

I wished for this girl's body.

A crash of thunder came in answer. It seemed to say AMEN!

As the rain eased, I followed Chris back across the field and said, 'You've no idea how lovely you looked as you danced back there.'

She turned and gave a bashful smile, her fun-bags firm and pointed. 'You're not so bad yourself,' she said, compressing her lips. But I wondered if she wasn't just being polite.

'I'd complement you on what you're wearing, but you haven't given me much to go on.'

Bending down, she picked a saturated dandelion, tapping it on her hand to fluff it up, and threaded it into her hair. I loved the way the moist down of her armpits contrasted with the smoothness of her breast.

'That's a *gorgeous* flower you're wearing.'

'I put it on just for you,' she said.

We walked along in silence, our bare feet squelching in the turf.

'You know what…?' I ventured. Her face evoked a cricketer straining for a difficult catch. 'I'm trained to give body massage. I've a pile of dry towels in my tent. Come back and get dry.'

For an instant she shivered. As the rain stopped, a chill breeze had sprung up, making it difficult for her to refuse. Kneeling on my groundsheet, she cautiously accepted a pink towel from the pile I dragged from my rucksack. I picked up another to pat her shoulders dry—and she let me.

Out came the baby powder. My dusted palms slipped over her skin like butter and she shut her eyes and groaned with passion. I pinioned her arms and our mouths coalesced, her moans buzzing on my lips like a bee snared in a web.

Witch camp is a many-body problem of astronomical complexity. Out of all the myriad possibilities, how were we to know that from the very outset her heavenly body had been on a collision course with mine?

*   *   *

'How can we have missed a thing that size?' said the director, eyes creased in anxious fury.

'Until last Sunday,' I explained, 'it was occulted by the planet Mars.' It was a lame excuse, but it happened to be true.

'So Mars just stepped aside… and there it was: coming straight at us?'

'And there it was,' I said. 'Full stop.'

'What was it that excited your suspicion?'

'I was doing measurements on M8. It got in my way.'

The director snorted, as if he was hoping I'd say something more impressive. 'Show me on the screen.'

I brought up yesterday's shot of Messier 8, aka the Lagoon Nebula in the constellation of Sagittarius, close to the galactic centre. It stood out clearly for me

159

because I knew what I was looking for, but it took him a while to see it.

But eventually he did. A patch of darkness in the field of stars. Those of course occur at random—but not circular patches.

He sat back with a sigh. 'You can't have been the only one to spot it. Hubble will show up every icicle.'

'Hubble's fully booked on Ultra Deep Field Five.'

'Mauna Kea, then. Palomar. Kitt Peak…'

'Not a peep out of any of them.'

The director swayed his head as if his nose was a windscreen wiper. 'Maybe they're just keeping mum. Think of the damage an inappropriate disclosure would do. Imagine the effect on the stock market, for a start…'

'I don't think the stock market's going to matter all that much.'

He looked at me in silence for several seconds. Then he bawled at me 'Are you absolutely certain of your calculations?'

'No one can be certain of anything yet. I'll have to rerun the program daily. Soon it will be hourly.'

His voice, when he spoke again, was scarcely audible. 'Will it really come to that?'

I shrugged. 'What do you want me to say?'

*　　*　　*

In the end we decided to keep it to ourselves. Let some other observatory be the first to report it. It was credit of a sort we didn't want.

It wasn't as if we could put our own names to the object. It had a name already. It had been observed fifteen years earlier in solar transit and designated X/1994 H5 (Schott-Ito)—from which an astronomer would infer that it was a comet of unknown trajectory discovered in the second half of April 1994, the fifth such object.

But Messrs Schott and Ito never got round to tracking it. Their funding was cut and it was lost. On its rediscovery, the IAU redesignated it A/1994 H5 (Schott-Ito), which emphasised that it was an asteroid mistaken for a comet. But to honour its original discoverers it was permitted to keep its cometary name.

This may serve to explain why we were in no rush to claim ownership, or rather, to own up to it. But then LINEAR, the Lincoln Near-Earth Asteroid Research project, announced it—and promptly awarded it 10 on the Torino scale.

Yes, you heard me correctly. Ten: the highest possible hazard rating. Then people started to ask how we'd managed to lose it in the first place.

All of this was in the future. But even then we knew more than we wanted to admit. Not enough, maybe, for us to go proclaiming doom from the housetops. But enough to start me, for one, liquidating my assets for what I could get for them.

I found a cash buyer for my Maidstone cottage pretty quickly and the sale was concluded with indecent haste. At that price, growled my agent, people would have scrambled to snap it up. But I knew it was the best price I was ever going to receive. I moved into a hotel: to hell with the cost. I knew it wasn't going to be for long.

I'd made a plan. Others would make plans too, once the news was out, but I was ahead of the field. I reckoned I'd have enough for a really good fortnight's holiday for two. Then I got on the phone to Chris.

Or more precisely, my hand was hovering over the phone when it rang. Chris it was that phoned me first.

'Have you heard the news?' she said. 'It's been on TV: every channel.'

'Chris,' I groaned, 'I work for the Royal Observatory. I *make* the news.'

A sharp inrush of breath. 'Then why is it me that's phoning you and not the other way round?'

What was she talking about? We hadn't been in touch since camp. Were we in a relationship, or weren't we? If not, then why did she suppose I'd think of phoning her, however earth-shattering the news?

But the fact was: *she* had phoned *me*… quite likely before she'd phoned anyone else. I abandoned my lofty position and decided it better to grovel.

'I was all set to,' I wailed. 'But you rang me first. Didn't you notice how quickly I answered?'

She took a moment to think about that—and I pressed home my advantage. 'Come away with me,

Chris. In my camper van: just the two of us. There's
no one else I want to spend my last few days with.'

Still she didn't speak.

'Why the hesitation? In a fortnight's time it won't
matter what we did, you and I. No one will care—or
even know—that we were in bed together the night
Schott-Ito came to earth…'

'The kids,' she blurted out. 'I'd love to, Dave, but
the kids need me.'

Kids?

Did she have a family, then? At camp she'd
seemed footloose and fancy-free. But you never could
tell. Not with anyone. The biggest talker of bullshine,
I'd chanced to discover, was a consultant surgeon in
ordinary life.

'Come round tomorrow morning,' she said.
'Seven-thirty if you can manage it. I'll let you meet
them.'

*   *   *

I rang her doorbell at 7.30 on the dot. She answered
the door in dark blue uniform with a watch pinned to
her breast pocket: the sort that only nurses wear.
Instead of inviting me in, she pushed past me and
opened the passenger door of her car. I got in and she
drove us off, out of the cul-de-sac and into the traffic
stream.

Everything was so mundane: the car, the traffic, the road. Were the last few days on earth going to be like any other?

Why not? Did anyone have a good idea for making them better days? If so, why hadn't it been done already?

On the other hand, if everything's about to end, why don't we just throw up our boring jobs right now? Fling care to the winds? Do whatever we fancy?

Well, that's all right for an individual, but it only works against the background of a world which keeps on going. And that means ordinary people staying on at their posts. The police must be on hand to prevent everything from collapsing in disorder. The shops must stay open to sell us food and clothing, even if we won't be needing those winter coats they've got in stock. The pumps must continue to deliver petrol, the banks to supply money, even though the accountants won't have to worry about balancing the books at the end of the month.

Here and there people went crazy and made themselves look stupid. But most of us had made the decision to go on living just as we were. So far as I knew, nobody apart from me was winding up their affairs to go on a joyride.

But even though I abandoned my home and private commitments, I didn't forsake my job. It so happened that, from being a state-sponsored luxury of no relevance to the lives of ordinary folk, I'd become the most important person on the planet. And as I had

predicted to my boss, I was indeed rerunning my
calculations hourly.

In the entire firmament that we astronomers used
to study, there was now just one celestial body that was
of any interest: a hundred-mile-wide ball of ice that
had been looping the sun for the past four-and-a-half
billion years. And would be perfectly happy to carry on
doing so for another four-and-a-half billion if only the
bloody Earth wasn't getting in the way.

Maybe Schott-Ito would miss us… and then how
silly we'd all look. At least, those of us who'd cashed in
our chips in the great game of life. But that wasn't the
reason everyone was breathing down my neck.

Where there's life there's hope, don't they say?
Where there's life there's choice, more like it. Right
now, I had no choice—and nor did anybody else.
That's what my calculations were saying. We were all
as good as dead.

That's why they used to put a black hood over
your head when they hanged you. Otherwise you'd
stare into the hangman's eyes right up to when he
dropped you through the trapdoor, looking for the
slightest sign he was about to relent. But there was no
hood big enough for our collective head. And no
chance that the hangman would relent.

It would have been better for it all to have been
played out in private, letting the world go to its death
in blissful ignorance. But I knew that in the actual hour
of collision there'd be only one programme going out
on all channels: the great white ball of Schott-Ito,

growing ever larger in the sky as it hurtled towards us at ninety-one thousand miles an hour, to deliver the energy of thirty thousand billion Hiroshimas. That's 4,411 nukes for every man, woman and child on the planet.

*　　*　　*

Chris stopped the car and we got out. We were in a hospital car park and she led me past railings and through corridors reminiscent of the House That Jack Built, until we stood in a bright airy ward with nursery pictures on the walls. A screaming child, if child it could be called (for it was almost my size) hurled itself at Chris, who caught it in her arms, barely managing to keep the pair of them upright.

'She's been like that since getting up, Sister,' a passing woman in white called out.

Sister?

'Ally, Ally,' cried Sister Chris. 'Calm down. What's wrong? Show me. Point.'

Ally was holding a rag ball of tie-bleached denim, crisp with dried spit, onto which torn patches of hessian had been stitched to make continents. If you half shut your eyes it was a fair likeness of the Earth, complete with clouds. Except it must have snagged on a nail because the stuffing was hanging out.

'Oh Ally! Your lovely ball!'

166

The child stopped screaming and settled into a steady drizzle of tears. Chris kissed her wet cheek and gave her a big hug.

'Sister will take it to her office and stitch it up again.'

I pondered that. Amid incoherent blubbing there had emerged evidence which could be acted upon to make things better for poor Ally, whose concerns were nearer home than a dirty great slushball still thirteen million miles away. Chris was doing far more good in her job than I was in mine.

'These are my children, Dave,' she said to me, as a nursing assistant led Ally back to the playroom. 'I can't go off and just leave them.'

*   *   *

Everyone was silent in the pub. There was a notice behind the bar stating that one particular topic was banned. Verboten. Taboo. The result was nobody had anything to talk about. Over our beers we watched TV in silence, eyes round with horror at events unfolding across the globe.

Burma filled the news that night. Not everybody was ready to go on living life as before. Some were determined to die in freedom—the cost no longer mattering. Hitherto the Army had been able to rule by fear. But now it was the Army, not the people, that had cause to be afraid. Trucks arriving at a neighbourhood to seize the residents were being overturned and set on fire. And the soldier staring through his gunsights at a charging mob knew that without a bullet for every one of those savage faces he was going to die—and never be missed.

I looked out of the window. Another glorious sunset. Was Mother Earth consoling her children in their last few days?

The truth was rather less poetic. Iran had thought it such a shame not to have the opportunity to use its precious nukes on the 'Zionist entity' that on Saturday, the Jewish Sabbath, it had taken out Tel Aviv. That same day, dead on 6pm as the Sabbath ended, Tehran had ascended to the stratosphere, spreading out to powder the globe in fine brown ash. The result of that nuclear spat was the most spectacular series of sunsets I could ever remember.

How could people hate each other so much as to begrudge their fellow men a final week of life? Or were they the lucky ones—to choose to go out in a blaze of glory? One that others could take note of, and appreciate?

Back home in little England, prophets of society's collapse looked like being proved wrong yet again. Other peoples' untempered response to unavoidable doom had brought it home to many that, hard though it was to carry on as usual, things could be far, far worse.

But how would folk behave when it was no longer days to go, but hours… then minutes?

I wept silently into my beer. I thought of the old man who had predicted the rainstorm: called it up, no less. They said at camp there was nothing he couldn't do... if you asked him nicely.

Why hadn't someone asked him to avert the catastrophe? Surely a man with meteorological powers could deflect a meteor?

And then it occurred to me: might it have been he who'd called it up in the first place? As punishment for our heedless rape of the Earth? I ought to pay him a visit. Say how sorry I was for all my wasteful habits and beg him to turn the asteroid aside. I vowed that if Schott-Ito missed us, I'd love the Earth and cherish it—and never throw away another plastic bag for the rest of my life.

And so my magical fantasies struggled with my scientific training. For hadn't I done the calculations myself? It was astrodynamics alone that governed the Earth's fate. Before ever a creature crept out of the sea, it had been 'in the stars', quite literally, that next Monday evening all life on Earth would stop.

*   *   *

Chris was working the graveyard shift: our off-duty times barely overlapped. We were getting a precious hour or two together, but all we did was lie in bed hugging each other. My wonderful scheme to zoom off into the sunset had wafted away like smoke. But I'd come up with no better plan to fill my remaining days.

In the space community, of which observatories like mine are the eyes and ears, I knew that people were working round the clock without a break. Rockets were being cobbled together and space capsules dragged out of museums. The aim was to launch every bit of space hardware that could possibly be brought back into service, to be in orbit at the moment Schott-Ito struck.

And then what?

Nobody had managed to explain it to me. After nearly seven billion souls had perished, for a year or two there'd still be a couple of dozen pairs of eyes to weep over the boiling earth. Then, pair by pair, the eyes would close… until all human experience became history: a history no one would ever read.

Just then a conversation going on behind my back intruded on my misery. There was talk amid chuckles of *spree, guns, hospital, rape* and *slaughter.* 'It'll be something to look forward to', I heard.

I glanced around. Those dismal words could have been coming from any of five groups of people sitting at the tables. I swivelled right round and stared about me. Nobody was talking.

It was at that moment the last of my illusions left me. *Something to look forward to.* Didn't that just sum it up? We know that death comes to us all in the end, but do we ever thread the implications into our lives… until it gets a booking in our diary?

My first response was to stand aghast at men planning to inflict atrocity upon their fellow beings, to no more enduring consequence than the last meal of a man due to be hanged. Just something to look forward to. But was I any different? Being more resourceful than the bastards I had overheard, though not as pragmatic, I'd planned for less repulsive delights to fill my last few days.

But all that had all depended on Chris's cooperation.

These louts knew something I didn't. If others were to play their part in my plans, they had to be compelled.

*   *   *

I didn't say anything about it to Chris. But once again I begged her to come away with me.

'Why does it have to be you that's on duty next Monday? Aren't things supposed to be carrying on as usual?'

'No, Dave, it's going to be like Christmas Day. It's not fair if some staff are on duty and others off, so we've all agreed to be on the ward for the last evening.'

'Chris,' I sobbed. 'Listen to me…'

'You'll come too, won't you, Dave? Oh Dave… please be there. For my sake.'

*   *   *

I knew then what I had to do. I sold my camper van and all the supplies I'd accumulated, and I bought

171

combat fatigues, an RPG-7 rocket launcher with two warheads, a Kalashnikov, an Uzi and boxes full of 9mm Parabellum rounds. I thought it would be difficult to buy, but no—it wasn't. On this Monday evening, the last Monday of all time, I have come to the hospital lugging it all.

Chris was horror-struck when she saw me. 'Dave—why are you dressed like that?' She'd spotted me through the window, beckoning to her to come outside. I hadn't wanted to go into the ward and scare everybody.

'You,' I said, 'have chosen of your own free will to be with your kids and comfort them right up to the last. I'm only sorry I can't be with you.'

'Why… why not?' She was shuddering visibly.

'I'm going to make sure the kids' last hour is a peaceful one. Full of love. Full of trust. And that means I've got to be on guard out here, hiding in the dark, in case certain people have other ideas.'

She stood there silently scrutinising my face. Then she slipped her arms round my neck. Tears glued our cheeks in a fragile bond. One kiss that was all too brief and back inside she went. Back into the light and the warmth, balloons and paper chains, and party hats perched on uncomprehending heads.

Meanwhile here I am outside, lying on a blanket as it all goes dark.

The sky is overcast. We won't see it coming after all. The TV spectacular won't take place now. Instead I guess they'll play old films dripping with nostalgia.

You'll only hear a boom to burst your head, as the sky goes brighter than you can imagine and the ground rucks up in a monstrous wave.

I shiver, staring into the deepening darkness through the sights of the rocket launcher. Not long to go now.

Where *are* they? I know they're coming. They'd better hurry up or they'll leave themselves no time for their little bit of fun.

So… come on, you bastards. *Really make my day!*

THE GIFT OF THE ANCESTORS

'In 24,000 years it will still be dangerous to live here.'
(Nuclear power worker, standing in the ruins of abandoned Pripyat)

I flay my sister and hang up her skin to dry. She weeps in my arms as my lapped stone cuts rivers in her tawny limbs. I kiss her blooded brow, assuring her of my love. As she bleeds on the outside, so I bleed within. She dies in my arms, and with unhurried tenderness I lay her in the grave we've dug that afternoon, and cover her with earth and fallen leaves.

Now surely won't the First Men be satisfied?

I do not want to do this thing, but how else can I turn aside their rage? The blood beneath our skin is the one thing of ours they want. They envy us for what they too once had—and have long since lost.

In the far north, so SunriseInTheNight tells me, it is so cold that people creep into the skins of bears they've slain. I shudder at the very notion. How can anyone put on the skin of someone not of their tribe: not already part of them, as my sister is of me? But SunriseInTheNight tells me I'm young and hasty: too quick to condemn, too slow to obey. Bitter cold drives men to horrid deeds. It forces them to come to terms with things they should abhor.

Do not destroy your enemy—so say the wise. Win him over. It gains you twice the spears and men needed to overcome him: those you have saved, plus all his own, which he would have hurled against you. Now he puts them at your disposal, or spends them in your interests.

That is how a man of the north wins over his foe, the bear. By putting on its skin he warms the bear to life again with his own life. He gives the bear blood once more—his own blood. And so the bear becomes his ally, not his foe. And, thus united, they go into the frozen forest, where a man alone could hardly go, to gather honey, nuts and branches.

What's with the branches, you may ask? Now here's the wonder of these people. Not only can they bring bears back to life as allies, but they can make an ally out of fire itself.

With fallen leaves, plus tar from lightning-struck trees, they actually hatch fire as they need it. In winter's frozen darkness they set fire to a hilltop then sit around the blaze, eating rotten apples for the bliss they bring.

The people of my tribe have no use for the skins of bears—creatures they dread. They have no use for fire, which they dread even more. Of all the elements, fire is the first to make war on, the last to befriend. Let a man fall into water, and once dry there is nothing to show for it. Let the wind blast him, but once warm there is nothing to be seen upon his skin.

Not so with fire. Fall into fire, or be so much as caressed by its fingers, and you are changed into a thing of horror till you die. In place of your smooth tawny skin you are given a stringy white dough, such as the mothers spit when they chew seeds for the sun-dried cakes we eat in winter. Dough that never feels like part of you. It is like mud, plastered on and dried. But scrape it off and you bleed to death, like my sister in my arms.

It is winter now. SunriseInTheNight is in the winter of his life. Soon, he tells me, he will go into the belly of Mother Earth, to re-emerge from the belly of Earth's daughters. Such a thing wipes a man clean of all that's gone before. As leaves fall to the ground and feed the trees, so men die and become the ancestors of their own children.

For how else can man go on bearing hurtful memories, heaped up in piles like leaves from years long past?

But some men die and come to life again without their memories wiped clean. SunriseInTheNight is such a one—that's why he is so precious to us. In his bygone life he journeyed far: even to the far north, where men do such horrid things. But one day, picking apples to dry in the sun, he fell and lay as dead for two whole moons. Then he awoke refreshed, as from a good night's sleep. He says he met the Ancestors—and has had long talks with them.

Alone of all the men I know, SunriseInTheNight does not fear death. I asked him if he'd always return to life that way, but he said no. Next time it will be as a small brown baby, his memory wiped clean as a licked bottom.

And so I learn all I can from him before he goes on that last journey. Nobody can understand why I sit in the cave listening to his ramblings, as they call it, when I could be outside, racing and wrestling in the warm sunbeams. But were I to repeat the wonders I've been hearing, the sun would beam on empty glades and I'd be squeezed out of the crush of listeners around the old man I've come to love.

What sort of wonders, you may ask?

Here's one. Alone of any man I know, SunriseInTheNight can make Artificial Fire. It is dangerous knowledge: CruelBear hates him for it. Some things, he says, should stay unknown until the day the sky falls in.

*　　*　　*

'StonyDawn—get outside with the other young men!'

CruelBear hauls me to my feet. But SunriseInTheNight thrusts out his hand and makes me sit back down beside him. CruelBear goes away muttering.

'Why must young men be wasted so?'

I tremble as I answer. 'The hyenas will come again tonight.' The old man snorts. 'Sheer nonsense!'

'Must we let hyenas eat us all?'

'It doesn't need young men to die. You and I alone, between us, we can keep the hyenas away.'

'How?'

'As it grows dark, let us make Fire before the cave mouth.'

*   *   *

The cave is the gift of Mother Earth. But we've had to fight for it. Hyenas used to dwell here. They still think of it as theirs—and they want it back. Each night they come in force to storm the cave. They tear our women's breasts and snatch away our babies. It is for us young men to sit in the dark outside the cave and offer our limbs to the hyenas' fangs: those we fail to strangle.

In winter, when our skins grow cold, CruelBear lets us young men sit inside the cave. It goes far back into the hillside. There is sweet water there in seeps and pools. It is never cold and never hot, but always stays the same. All winter long our skins do not dry out and sores begin to grow. But we prefer that to putting on the skins of bears, or risking being turned to stringy dough by fire.

The sun goes down behind the birch tops. SunriseInTheNight squats down to unwrap his squirrel skin of rosin flakes, dry leaves and stones. Soon the darkening sky is outshone by fresh young flames, and the old man calls for fallen branches. These the young men bring him and he feeds them to the fire, or uses

179

them to beat down flames as they try to escape. He orders them as if they were his children. And so we have another name for him: FireFather.

Hyenas do not trouble us this night. No one has to die, or lose a limb. But some complain it is unnatural. Young men are there to give their limbs for the tribe. And men have lived through winters past without making common cause with fire: the enemy alike of man and hyena.

*   *   *

Then that took place which has angered the Ancestors so.

GushingCleft, my mother, was once strong and fair. But now her breath is short and her limbs are as dead branches. Inside the cave she lies and shudders on a heap of leaves. The world for her is full of cold and empty of all else. I and my brothers take turns to lie hugging her. CruelBear won't let us carry fire into the cave: not even in the form of heated stones. And so my mother shudders on her heap of leaves.

SunriseInTheNight saw my grief and turned it into hope.

'Way to the south of here, in the middle of a bitter desert, there is a mountain range that stands out like this vein on the back of my hand.'

I stared, and as I did so his hand became a bitter desert. The vein rose through the shimmering air to

180

become a lofty mountain range, with crests of sunbeams and hollows of blue shadow.

'In that mountain there is a cave. Not a natural cave, but one made by the hands of men.'

I'm gripped with terror. 'However can that be?'

'You've seen Artificial Fire. Why can't there be Artificial Caves?'

'None but the First Men could have made such things!'

'It was indeed the First Men who made this.'

'How?'

The old man paused and rolled his eyes, as he did when storytelling. 'They did it when the mountain was still soft: fresh-spewed onto the earth as from a slit belly. They had a giant member. This they dipped in water… and poked.' He thrust out with his finger, and with his lips he made a noise like breaking wind.

'To the left and to the right the cave branches, like fish bones. At the end of each branch there are stacks and stacks of grey logs. Each log is smooth as ice, or as a stone polished in the river. Each log is exactly like another. The logs never move, for they are covered in dust and cobwebs. But each log… is alive!'

My fingers bit into his arm like hawkish talons. But he showed no sign of noticing. Together we were far away, standing in a terrifying cave, in a lofty mountain range, in a bitter desert, as he pointed out to me what he saw with the eyes of his bygone life.

'Each log,' he says, 'is the length of a man's body. And like a man's body it is warm to the touch. But unlike a man it never dies. For is it not hundreds of lives of men since it was laid down in the cave—and still it's warm to the touch?'

Realisation strikes me and I gasp. 'Suppose we had one of those wonderful logs! CruelBear would have no qualms about letting it in the cave. He'd think it safe and warm as a living body.'

'Just so,' says SunriseInTheNight. 'And GushingCleft could have it to embrace, like the men she used to love.' He let out a sigh.

Suddenly I saw the purpose of my life. 'Father, I will fetch one of these wonderful logs for GushingCleft to hug, like the men she used to love. I will fetch it as a gift from the Ancestors.'

*   *   *

Next day I sought out my brother MadBull and told him my idea. In one eye I saw lust kindled for adventure, but in the other I saw he thought me crazy. But arm-in-arm we went to CruelBear. 'Yes, go,' he said. 'You'll be no great loss to the tribe. But MadBull will, so he must stay.'

MadBull replied that he too must go, else who would bring his brother safely home? CruelBear turned his back, saying we could both go.

To my surprise and joy SunriseInTheNight said he was coming too. 'For how else will you find the Mountain, and the Cave?'

'A mountain should not be too hard to find.'

'And the Cave?'

*   *   *

The cold fresh air and the snow on the ground charged
the old man with vigour. He laughed like a boy and
leapt about as we began our journey. 'How glad I am
to be out of that stuffy cave.'

A blackbird flew down to a branch jutting out over
the path. '*Pui-pui diddia chiu ch-dik!*'

Putting out both hands, the old man made us halt.
He replied without hesitation, '*pui-pui lia tui?*'

'*Yup-ieh M'zzzia peeh pori: geveeah pur quis-quis!*' The
bird flew off.

'What did he say?' Neither MadBull nor I had
spent much time chatting with birds, leaving it to
others to tell us if they had anything important to say.
The arrogance of youth.

'He says there's an angry bear in the woods that's
been stung on the nose by a bee, and that we would do
well to go carefully.'

We carried on walking in silence, and with greater
awareness of our surroundings.

As the sun went down SunriseInTheNight made
Fire to keep us warm and safe from bears.

'Fire is no danger if made on a hilltop. With due
care we can stop the trees catching fire and setting the
woods ablaze.' To that end he sent us to fetch water in
our deerskins.

183

He taught us to curb the baby fire and carefully feed it. Like a tame wolf cub it became docile and obedient. I called it LittleFire, but it would not answer to its name. Then again, did I really want it to follow me everywhere?

In the heart of the night, the old man woke me up. MadBull was already sitting by the drowsy fire, dropping tiny twigs on it, which cracked and flared.

Far to the north the land was burning with a pale green cloudy fire. On the horizon stood a hidden cliff, over which the green fire tumbled in waves.

'That is my sunrise in the night. When I came back from the dead, I saw fit to take it as my name.'

'Is it fire—or water?'

'It is fire, of a sort.'

But for an instant I saw a flayed skin hung on a branch, turning slowly in the breeze.

He carried on. 'Not like the fire I made tonight. It is too far away to reach on foot. No matter how far north you journey, you cannot come at last to stand beneath the glowing waterfall.'

And by those words I knew that he had tried.

He bade us turn our faces towards the stars. 'They too are fire.'

'Like sparks from our blaze?'

MadBull joined in. 'Like fireflies in the forest?'

'Neither. Each tiny speck is a whole forest ablaze in itself. Very large and very bright.'

I thought he was teasing. 'How can you possibly credit such a thing?'

'I don't have to credit it. I can see it with my own eyes.'

'How?'

'As we walk in the woods, have you noticed how the trunks of the nearer trees drift behind us faster than those farther off? That doesn't happen with the stars, no matter how far you go. So must they not be very far away? Further away even than that green fire? But think of this: to be able to see one single star at such a distance, must it not be very big and bright?'

But MadBull wasn't having it. 'Stars are not like the trunks of trees. My mother said they floated on the sky like leaves on a dark pond.'

'An upside-down pond?'

As I listened to them argue, I said within my heart: they are both wrong. Had I not seen the sparks swirl up from our bonfire? Had they not then merged with the stars? How could stars be anything but sparks? From every fire in the world. Even from that green fire in the North.

But I marvelled that the same sight could look so different to the three of us. Was it something to do with our eyes? My eyes are hazel and my brother's brown. The old man's eyes are blue. Why cast about for any other cause?

*　*　*

In the morning, near our camp, we found a dead hare. It had been freshly killed by wolves, but they had made

no show of eating it. Had the nearness of the fire
poisoned it—and was that something they could tell?

'No, it's tribute. "Stay right there," the wolves are
saying, "and we will feed you and keep you free from
harm."'

'Can wolves be bearing us such goodwill?'

'Why not? See here: we are camped across an
animal trail, barring escape for their prey.'

'Do the wolves seek to make tame beasts of us, as
we do of fire?'

'Allies, let us say.'

He took up the dead hare, skinned it and spitted it,
holding it over the rekindled embers. This was
something I had not seen done before.

MadBull spoke with disapproval. 'Never eat
anything you haven't killed yourself. So say the Elders.
There is poison in the fangs of wolves.'

'This meat will be all right. The fire will cleanse it.
Anyway I see no marks of fangs.'

Presently a reek arose as I had only ever smelled
on women's bodies. And so we broke our fast on
strange delightful food.

*　　*　　*

We travelled south along a great river, its muddy
waters warm upon our skins as we clung to logs or
tried to sit astride them. Fierce lizards basked on the
muddy banks. Occasionally they slipped into the water
and vanished. They terrified me—how was I to see

186

one before it was upon me? But SunriseInTheNight said that what we cannot guard against we should not fear. Fear exists only to help us stay alive. If that is something we have no power over, what purpose does fear serve?

Within three moons we were in a bitter desert. The ground was white dust: it cracked the skin of our feet and made them sore. On the horizon mountains marched in a line. One of them was ours, and soon we saw the mouth of the cave the old man had known was there. He made us gather armfuls of dry rushes, and from these he twisted dollies as you give to children. Taking three, to each he set a flame of Artificial Fire. My chest was tight and my mouth was dry. But in we went, crowding close together.

As each dolly burnt down, we lit another from it. Fire itself became our friendly guide. Soon we came across the wonderful logs the old man had described. We tipped one on its side, and as it fell it spoke one word in song. We rolled it across the amazingly flat ground to the mouth of the cave. Once in daylight, we stared at it hard.

It was grey and shiny, rather like a fish. There were no marks upon it save two, impossible to miss. Not natural marks but deliberate ones, such as pumas scratch on trees.

The first mark was puzzling. It was a kind of yellow leaf—a trefoil rimmed in black—a canker on the pure skin of an apricot. But there was nothing puzzling about the second mark: it was a skull.

MadBull scratched his ear. 'Has this been cut from the trunk of a ghost tree? Or has it been fashioned by living men?'

'By men while still alive, though now long dead.'

'Having made it perfect, why did they mar it with these two wounds?'

'Why is a man tattooed, but as a mark of dedication?'

'Dedication… to what?'

SunriseInTheNight waved his hand, as if repelling flies. 'How should I know? Am I one of the First Men?'

But MadBull wasn't settling for that. Something was worrying him.

'What do you suppose they mean?'

The old man stood up, clutching his wisp of a beard. It struck me he'd not anticipated such a question. But I've never known him stumped for an answer. Once more the storyteller, he rolled his eyes.

'The skull is a smile from a man long dead. He is, after all, an ancestor of ours. So how could he ever mean us harm? The yellow tattoo is the sun, with three sunbeams radiating life, health and warmth.'

MadBull grinned and nodded, reassured. But for an instant I saw—not three sunbeams—but three axe heads stained with ashy darkness.

*　　*　　*

188

After we forsook the Cave, SunriseInTheNight fell ill.
But he refused to let us carry the log by ourselves,
taking his turn to shoulder it.

He staggered on until he collapsed and we took it
from him. When we got to the great river his eyes were
red and swollen. He seemed not to be seeing the things
around him.

That night he died.

We did not throw his body in the river, nor leave it
for the wolves to eat. Unwise to give a foretaste of
ourselves to anything that might be tracking us. That
evening, by mute and mutual agreement, we laid his
body on the fire that was his art, and covered it with
fallen branches. Then we watched his life fly up in
sparks among the stars. The flames leapt so high that
the leaves on boughs above us grew old and flared
away. But we had little concern for the woods that
night.

*   *   *

The journey back took longer. We could not ride the
river, for now it flowed the wrong way. Our progress
grew harder than mere distance would explain. A great
sadness had fallen upon us. Our feet dragged in the
dirt and sickness ate us up inside. Great sores began to
flourish on our backs, as if we'd fallen into fire. Then
we began to lose our hair. I noticed it first with my
brother. Soon our chests grew bare as bones, and our
heads became like polished pebbles in a stream. Our

bowels started to run with green slime streaked with red, as if we were fruits rotting away inside.

At night it was beyond our strength to make a fire as he had taught us. But now we had the precious log to hug. How warm and comforting it was! When I closed my eyes I could still see sparks from the fire. Like shooting stars they stabbed the darkness of my inner sky.

We told each other not to fear the wolves, for we had no strength to defend ourselves. So what was the use of fear? But of wolves we saw no trace. Perhaps they sensed the ill upon us—as did our tribe when we got home.

*　　*　　*

At length we came to a place where I knew every tree. As we drew near our cave, our tribe with shrieks of joy came running out to meet us. But when they reached us they recoiled in horror.

CruelBear would not let us in the cave. He said we'd picked up some disease on our journey. So we camped out in the open air with no fear of hyenas, as we had done for over half a year. A few young braves—a very few—came to sit beside our fire and hear how SunriseInTheNight had met his end.

The precious log enjoyed a better welcome. Still warm, like mother's breasts, it felt so safe and kind, radiating pure goodness. With joy I watched it carried in the cave. Soon CruelBear came to us with a conceding shrug.

'GushingCleft demands to see you both. But don't stay long.'

Reaching out to us and grasping our arms with twig-like fingers, she sang her blessings on us both. The whole time we'd been away nobody had made a fire, of course. So lots of children had been lost to the hyenas. Now all that was going to stop. Had SunriseInTheNight stolen fire from the First Men on our behalf, just to lie in ashes in the woods?

*　*　*

When evening came I lit a fire before the cave, and all night long I sat and tended it. High in the sky I saw them plainly: sparks from the old man's pyre. I thought of the First Men, who had poked holes in the mountainside as a boy pokes clay. They must have known of fire and all its hazards, and set their hearts on finding something safer. Safe enough to give your dying mother to warm her feeble limbs. And as a fond bequest to their descendants, they'd built a formidable cave to last forever, filled with these wonderful logs.

In summers to come, our young men will go back for more. They will travel the world, giving them to other tribes. Why should we keep them to ourselves? That's not the way mankind will ever flourish.

But it seems the First Men don't want us to flourish. One after another, folk fall prey to weird disease. CruelBear says it only began on our return. Was it because of our audacious theft? Or did we disturb their ghosts as we explored their cave? They've made us send them my lovely sister as peacemaker. They'll not be satisfied with that: they'll want me too.

MadBull expired just half a moon ago. I shall not survive him long. Once everyone has gone who dared this venture, then surely the First Men must forget their anger, and leave us in peace to enjoy our prize?

My mother lived for just three days after we brought her the gift of the Ancestors. But I don't begrudge the effort in the least. Her final days were spent in warmth and comfort. I too, in my turn, will die hugging the shining log. Then may it stand forever at the cave's centre, a warm living heart to guard my tribe, while any of us yet remain.

www.ingramcontent.com/pod-product-compliance
Lightning Source LLC
Chambersburg PA
CBHW020810190726
48285CB00006B/2224